You're About to Become a
Privileged
Woman.

INTRODUCING
PAGES & PRIVILEGES™.

It's our way of thanking you for buying
our books at your favorite retail store.

*Get All This **Free***
WITH JUST ONE PROOF OF PURCHASE:

◆ **Hotel Discounts** up
to 60% at home and
abroad ◆ **Travel Service**
- Guaranteed lowest
published airfares
plus 5% cash back

$50 VALUE

on tickets ◆ **$25 Travel Voucher**
◆ **Sensuous Petite Parfumerie** collection

◆ **Insider Tips Letter**
with sneak previews

You'll get a
It's your passpo
even more great

There's no club to join. No purchase commitment. No obligation.

Enrollment Form

☐ *Yes!* I WANT TO BE A *Privileged Woman.*

Enclosed is one *PAGES & PRIVILEGES*™ Proof of Purchase from any Harlequin or Silhouette book currently for sale in stores (Proofs of Purchase are found on the back pages of books) and the store cash register receipt. Please enroll me in *PAGES & PRIVILEGES*™. Send my Welcome Kit and FREE Gifts -- and activate my FREE benefits -- immediately.

More great gifts and benefits to come like these luxurious Truly Lace and L'Effleur gift baskets.

NAME (please print)

ADDRESS   APT. NO

CITY   STATE   ZIP/POSTAL CODE

PROOF OF PURCHASE

Please allow 6-8 weeks for delivery. Quantities are limited. We reserve the right to substitute items. Enroll before October 31, 1995 and receive one full year of benefits.

**NO CLUB!
NO COMMITMENT!**
Just one purchase brings you great Free Gifts and Benefits!
(More details in back of this book.)

Name of store where this book was purchased_____

Date of purchase_____

Type of store:

☐ Bookstore   ☐ Supermarket   ☐ Drugstore

☐ Dept. or discount store (e.g. K-Mart or Walmart)

☐ Other (specify)_____

Which Harlequin or Silhouette series do you usually read?

_____

Complete and mail with one Proof of Purchase and store receipt to:

U.S.: *PAGES & PRIVILEGES*™, P.O. Box 1960, Danbury, CT 06813-1960

Canada: *PAGES & PRIVILEGES*™, 49-6A The Donway West, P.O. 813, North York, ON M3C 2E8   **PRINTED IN U.S.A**

Luke Thought That Cows Had It Better.

No one told them they had to move right when they were in the throes of delivery. No one hustled them from bed to gurney to delivery table. But then, no cow, to his knowledge, had ever had Jill to help her through it. And Jill was an asset, no doubt about it.

She steadied the woman by her mere presence. She spoke calmly and soothingly all the while the doctor and nurses did their bit. Luke watched. And felt as useless and out of place as a steer in a pen full of heifers. He wasn't sure exactly when the faint, queasy feeling turned into something a little more pressing. He took a desperate step back toward the wall.

"Oh, hell," he heard the doc mutter. "Get him outta here."

The next thing he knew he was in the corridor, sitting in a chair with Jill next to him. He dragged in air, felt himself shudder, heard the rushing sound in his ears fade gradually. He stared down at the blue gauze sanitary shoes they'd made him put on over his mud-caked boots. In the distance he heard a baby crying....

Dear Reader,

Imagine that you're single, and you've been longing for a family all your life…but there aren't any husband prospects in sight. Then suddenly, a handsome, sexy rancher offers you a proposition: marry him. The catch—you've got to help raise his four rambunctious children. It's tempting…but is it practical? That's the dilemma faced by Kara Kirby in this month's MAN OF THE MONTH, *The Wilde Bunch* by Barbara Boswell. What does Kara do? I'm not telling—you have to read the book!

And a new miniseries begins, MEN OF THE BLACK WATCH, with *Heart of the Hunter* by BJ James. The "Black Watch" is a top-secret organization whose agents face danger every day, but now face danger of a different sort—the danger of losing your heart when you fall in love.

In addition, the CODE OF THE WEST series continues with Luke's story in *Cowboys Don't Quit* by Anne McAllister. And the HEART OF STONE series continues with *Texas Temptation* by Barbara McCauley.

For a light, romantic romp don't miss Karen Leabo's *Man Overboard;* and a single dad gets saddled with a batch of babies in *The Rancher and the Redhead* by Suzannah Davis.

I hope you enjoy them all—I certainly do!

Lucia Macro
Senior Editor

Please address questions and book requests to:
Silhouette Reader Service
U.S.: 3010 Walden Ave., P.O. Box 1325, Buffalo, NY 14269
Canadian: P.O. Box 609, Fort Erie, Ont. L2A 5X3

ANNE McALLISTER
COWBOYS DON'T QUIT

To Donna
Best always,
Anne McAllister

SILHOUETTE *Desire*®
Published by Silhouette Books
America's Publisher of Contemporary Romance

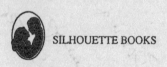

SILHOUETTE BOOKS

ISBN 0-373-05944-2

COWBOYS DON'T QUIT

Printed in U.S.A.

Books by Anne McAllister

Silhouette Desire

Cowboys Don't Cry #907
Cowboys Don't Quit #944

*Code of the West

ANNE McALLISTER

was born and raised in California, land of surfers, swimmers and beach-volleyball players. She spent her teenage years researching them in hopes of finding the perfect hero. It turned out, however, that a few summer weeks spent at her grandparents' in Colorado and all those hours in junior high spent watching Robert Fuller playing Jess Harper on "Laramie" were formative. She was fixated on dark, handsome, intense, lone-wolf types. Twenty-six years ago she found the perfect one prowling the stacks of the university library and married him. They now have four children, three dogs, a fat cat and live in the Midwest (as in "Is this heaven?" "No, it's Iowa.") in a reasonable facsimile of semiperfect wedded bliss to which she always returns—even though the last time she was in California she had lunch with Robert Fuller.

Cowboys Don't Cry and *Cowboys Don't Quit* are the first two books in a three-book series about the Tanner brothers. Watch for Noah's story in *Cowboys Don't Stay,* coming to you in December.

One

He was dreaming again.

The same dream. Always the same. They were body-surfing near the pier at Manhattan Beach, he and Keith—laughing, joking, competing as always for the biggest wave, the steepest drop, the longest ride.

They were showing off for Keith's fans on the pier, all of them watching, waving, smiling.

He saw Jillian, Keith's fiancée, there, braced against the railing, her long dark hair tangling across her face in the wind as she waved to Keith, then looked out to sea and pointed.

They both looked back toward where she was indicating. The swell was already noticeable, building now, moving toward them.

"Wave of the day!" Keith yelled, grinning and moving into position, beginning to stroke toward shore.

Luke watched Keith go, then he moved too, slower, as he always was in the water, but still in time. He caught the momentum, merging with the force of the wave, rising on its crest to see the water and the foam and the beach spread out before him. He caught a glimpse of Jillian leaning over the railing, watching intently. He spied Keith just ahead, already into the fall.

And then he fell, too, as the wave crested, curving under, dropping him headlong into the backwater. It pounded down on top of him, pressing him into the ocean floor even as it dragged him along. He felt a thump. His body collided with Keith's. Arms and legs tangled in the power of the wave. They struggled, shifted, separated. He felt Keith's fingers grab for him. They clutched, touched, clung, oddly frantic. And then they slipped away.

Away...

He opened his mouth to call. *Keith!*

But the water choked him. Gagged him. Pressed down upon him, swirling and pounding, grinding him into the sand, crushing his lungs, burning his throat.... Then for a moment, blessed air. And just as suddenly the wet suffocation was back, choking him, covering his nose....

Luke jerked awake. Hank, the old herding dog, was licking his face.

"Damn." He shuddered and pushed her away. "Hell of a way to say good mornin'," he grumbled, but he knew it wasn't Hank's fault. It was the dream.

Always and, it seemed, forever—the dream. And that wasn't even the way it had happened, for God's sake.

It—Keith's death.

Even now, almost two years later, it was hard to think of Keith Mallory as dead. Intense, dynamic, irrepressible Keith—mover and shaker, dreamer and doer, one of

America's best-loved actors, not to mention Luke's own best friend—had always had more to live for, more to give than anyone he knew.

Luke's fists clenched futilely against the lingering feel of Keith's fingers slipping out of his grasp. He drew a ragged breath.

In reality he'd had no chance to come that close.

He hadn't even been in the water. He'd been standing high and dry on the riverbank, too far away to help, yet too near not to realize what was happening.

Luke sat up on his cot now, shivering not so much from the cold as from the memory. He dragged in another breath of the crisp Colorado mountain air and tried to shake off the shivers. But even though it was already July, at close to nine thousand feet it never got very warm until the sun was up, and what memories didn't accomplish, the cool morning temperature did.

He pulled his knees up to his chest and wrapped his arms around them, his body trembling in a now-familiar cold sweat. He rubbed a hand across his wet face, tasting salt amid the dog slobber. Tears. He rested his head against his bent knees and tried to steady his breathing.

Keith. Oh, God, Keith, I'm sorry. It should have been me.

The dog nudged his shoulder and tried to lick him again. Luke looped an arm around her neck and rubbed his face against her fur. Then he scrubbed a hand across his eyes and hauled himself to his feet. There would be no sleeping now, no point in even trying.

Not that he wanted to. Not when he dreamed.

He could tell from the faint light filtering through the window of the rough log cabin that it wasn't quite dawn. The sky to the east was still more dark gray than rose. But there was nothing to be gained by staying in bed; he would just lie there remembering what he would give his soul to forget.

He picked up the coffeepot, let himself out into the chill mountain air and headed toward the spring. He filled the pot, then carried it back to the cabin, dumped in some coffee and started a fire on the small propane stove.

He made himself concentrate on each task as he performed it. Whatever part of his mind he didn't keep firmly focused on what he was doing would be on the dream or, worse, on the memories that caused it.

He rubbed his fingers together. He couldn't feel the clutch of Keith's fingers anymore. Sometimes the sensation lasted for hours. Not today, thank God.

While the coffee was heating, he scrubbed his face with some of the water he'd brought up the night before, then dragged a comb through his shaggy dark hair. He could tell by feel that the next time he went into town he'd better stop by Bernie's and get a haircut. Not that he'd be going anytime soon. Lots of camp men these days came down off the summer range every week or so, but they had friends, family, people to see, mail to pick up, a life to keep in touch with in town.

Luke didn't. Nor did he want any. He set his hat on his head and tugged down the brim, then went back to the stove.

The coffee was hot. He poured himself a mugful and stood staring out the small window, making himself think about what he needed to do that day. Bring cattle up out of the creek bottom—that was a given. They were like magnets, those cows. You barely got them up to the head of the draw and left them, when they drifted right back down again. Or got spooked and ran back. He needed to circle up the mountain and check on the cattle near the national-forest land, making sure the gates were closed. Hikers didn't seem to realize all the work they caused when they didn't leave gates the way they found them. If even one gate had been left open, he'd have his day's work cut out for him.

In the early morning light he could look down across the meadow and see three of his horses already lurking by the quaky fence, waiting for him to holler them down and grain them. He didn't even need to holler anymore. He'd been doing it for more than a year now—long enough that they knew what to expect.

He took another swallow of coffee, then set his cup down and got out food for the dogs. There were two others besides Hank—a scruffy-looking catch dog called Muff and another Border collie named Tommy. They brushed against his legs as he poured their food out for them. Hank nudged his hand, her pointy noise wet and cold against his fingers. Luke rubbed her under the chin.

The panic was gone now. The pressure had eased on his lungs as the dream faded, and sunrise brought light, clarity and color to the mountain meadow he called home.

Breathing more steadily now, Luke finished his cup of coffee. He made and ate a quick breakfast, then set to work.

Some days entailed more work than others. Luke liked the work. He sought it, needed it, created it. Today, because of the dream, he made even more than there was.

He moved twenty head of cattle out of the creek bottom, doctored some foot rot and rode the fence along the national-forest line. The gates were all closed, but someone had cut the wire to get through where there wasn't one.

He rounded up a dozen cattle and brought them back down, fixed the fence, then circled through a stand of aspen toward the creek. And found one of his young bulls caught in the middle of a willow patch.

Bulls weren't the easiest critters to deal with at the best of times, and when they'd been stuck as long as this bull had likely been, their tempers weren't exactly sweet. This fellow was no exception.

Luke was tempted to leave him. Nobody was looking over his shoulder, and it was his bull. But the bull couldn't do his job unless Luke did his. More than that, though, Luke knew a dreamless sleep came only when he was so dead tired he couldn't move.

He laid a loop over the bull's head, alternately dragging on the rope and urging the animal forward, while Hank and Tommy nipped and prodded. He was doing his whooping and hollering on foot, not on horseback, when the bull finally broke free and rewarded him with a kick at his ribs.

He missed. But that's when Luke discovered the bull had foot rot.

"Son of a gun," he muttered, taking off his hat to wipe a hand through sweat dampened hair. "Must be my lucky day."

He was dirty and sweaty, tired and sore by the time he rode back over the rise that looked down on his camp. The bull might've missed Luke's ribs with that first kick, but he hadn't missed his shin later when Luke was maneuvering his horse in close enough to give the animal an injection.

Luke figured he'd be hobbling tomorrow. He didn't care. Physical pain wouldn't keep him awake or make him dream.

Tonight he'd earned his sleep, and he thought he just might get it, too.

Until he saw someone sitting by his cabin door.

Nobody he'd invited, that was damn certain. Since he'd moved up the mountain a year ago last spring, Luke hadn't encouraged visitors. Jimmy, his hand, who was renting Luke's ranch house, came up whenever Luke asked him to help move cattle or to bring salt, and now and then he brought Luke provisions or a coffee cake or some cookies his wife, Annette, had made. But Jimmy had just been up three days ago. And Luke's only other visitor was his old schoolmate Linda Gutierrez's son, Paco.

"You don't want him around, you send him away," Linda had told him from the first.

But Luke knew Paco's dad had died three years ago, and he remembered all too well how he'd felt when his own dad had died. He'd been older than Paco when it happened—sixteen. Paco was only eight and needier even than he had been.

Luke hadn't had the heart to send the boy away.

Besides, talking with Paco was a form of penance. All the kid ever wanted to do was hear about Keith. He probably knew by heart every movie Keith Mallory had made, and he took great joy in asking Luke about the ones he'd worked on.

Luke wondered when he'd realize that it was his fault the boy's hero was dead.

He sat up a little straighter in the saddle now, trying to guess his visitor's identity. Whoever it was saw him and got up, beginning to move toward him now.

It was a woman.

A tall and slender woman in jeans that hugged curves no cowboy'd ever have. Long brown hair tangled across

her face in the evening breeze. Then the breeze lifted the
swath of hair and Luke felt as if the bull had kicked him
right in the gut.

God, no! It couldn't be.

He shut his eyes, begged and pleaded with the Almighty. Then he opened them again, still praying.

To no avail.

It was Jillian. Jillian Crane.

Luke wished the earth would open and swallow him
up.

No such luck.

He slowed his horse, tempted to turn tail and head
right back up the mountain, knowing damned well he
would have if she hadn't seen him. But she had, so he had
no choice but to continue down.

He didn't know what the hell she was doing here.
Couldn't begin to imagine. They hadn't seen each other
since the day of Keith's funeral, almost two years ago.

They hadn't spoken even then.

They hadn't needed to.

Jill had said everything there was to say the afternoon
Keith died.

Luke could remember it as clearly as if it had been
yesterday. It had haunted him so often that it might as
well have been. . . .

They'd been two weeks into a new movie, a tough-guy,
mountain-man script with lots of the action-adventure
stuff that was Keith's forte and his stunt-double Luke's
bread and butter. It was grueling, strenuous and more
than a little dangerous—exactly the sort of thing they
both loved.

They'd been filming for fourteen days straight from a
gritty little town on the Salmon River in Idaho, and by

the end of the second week in October they were as gritty, earthy and wild looking as the landscape.

It was still warm during the days, but chilly after the sun went down, and every night after they finished, he and Keith and some of the rest of the crew would warm their insides in the local bar.

They were a few beers into the warming process, throwing darts and arguing about which of them was the better shot—and hence the better man—when Luke stepped up to take his toss.

Suddenly the door opened . . . and there she was.

Jillian.

His dart sailed over the top of the board.

If anyone noticed, it wasn't Keith.

"Hey," Keith had shouted, a sudden, broad grin lighting his unshaven face. "My lady's come!" And he knocked over a bar stool in his haste to get to her.

Luke didn't move. He stood rooted to the spot, watching as Keith wrapped Jill in a bear hug, then turned, grinning, his arm looped over her shoulders, and faced the rest of them.

"Look who's here," he said unnecessarily.

"Bring 'er on over," one of the sound men had called out. "Plenty of room, ain't that right, Luke?"

For a moment, Luke didn't speak. Couldn't. He wasn't prepared. *So, get prepared,* he commanded himself. He drew a deep, steadying breath, met Keith's grin, then let his eyes settle on Jill. "That's right," he said.

Keith just shook his head. "Not on your life. Come on, sweetheart." He started to draw Jill with him toward the door, then stopped and kissed her long and hard, surfacing only long enough to glance over his shoulder at them and say, "Find your own women to keep you warm." Then he dragged her off to his room.

Their room, Luke corrected himself.

The one right on the other side of the wall from his.

Not that he went back to his. He had no intention of lying there in his cold, solitary bed and thinking about Keith making love to Jill at that very moment on the other side of a few inches of plaster.

Because that's what Keith would be doing.

It's what Luke would be doing if Jill were his. But she wasn't. Would never be.

A man didn't poach on his best friend's girl.

A man got drunk instead.

He didn't go back to his room until after two the next morning. He stayed out as long as the bars stayed open. But even when he got back, drunk and dead tired, he still didn't sleep.

He lay there listening for the slightest noise, the softest murmur, the faintest rustling sound from the bed in the next room. He heard nothing. It didn't matter; his imagination was enough. He finished his bottle of whiskey only an hour before his alarm went off in the morning.

He made it to the set on time, but his bloodshot eyes and haggard face were a dead giveaway.

"Little too much celebrating?" Keith was in high good humor as he teased Luke about his hangover.

And why wouldn't he be? Luke thought savagely. He barely grunted a reply.

"Oughta get yourself a lady like mine," Keith told him cheerfully. "You wouldn't be out runnin' around if you had yourself a Jill."

For an instant Luke's eyes met Jill's. At once she looked away.

"Oh, for heaven's sake, Keith. Leave him alone," she said irritably, taking his hand. "Luke doesn't want an old stick-in-the-mud like me."

"He'd better not. You're mine." Keith grinned at her and punched Luke lightly on the arm. "C'mon. Grab some coffee and let's get this show on the road."

They were set up to shoot the scene where Keith's character, a renegade cowboy, escaped from a band of Indian pursuers, hurtling down a draw to where he'd left his canoe. Then, under a barrage of arrows, he was supposed to shove off, jump into the canoe and paddle into the roiling river while the white water swept him out of sight.

"We've got it almost all rigged," Carl Oakes, the stunt coordinator, said to Luke when he and Keith found him on the riverbank. "Plenty of safety lines, so if things look grim, bail out."

Luke nodded. He swallowed, studying the tumbling white water, trying to psyche himself up. His head pounded, and his stomach was roiling worse than the river.

"I want to do it," Keith said suddenly.

Luke jerked his head around to see the determined set of his friend's jaw.

Carl rolled his eyes. "Don't be an idiot. That's what Luke's here for. He's the stuntman. You're the star."

Keith nodded. "Exactly. That's the point." And Luke could see him getting psyched up even as he spoke. "It's me that people want to see do it."

"You just want Jill to see you do it," Carl said, with a wink at Luke.

Luke didn't say anything.

Keith grinned. "Well, that, too."

"Garrison won't let you," Carl predicted. "No way he's going to let you."

But surprisingly, Garrison, the director, was willing to listen to Keith's argument. He even agreed that shooting

Keith in close-up as he scrambled into the canoe, then panning wide as he moved downstream, was a good idea.

"No break, huh? Makes sense," he said, a speculative smile forming. "It's not too big a risk, is it?" He looked at Carl for confirmation.

Keith scoffed. "Carl's more careful than my mother. Aren'tcha, Carl?"

Carl scowled and muttered under his breath. But Keith kept talking and Garrison kept listening, while Luke stood by, wishing he was a million miles away, and didn't say a word.

He knew what was going to happen. He'd seen it before. It wasn't just showing off for Jill, though Luke knew—and Keith knew—that was part of it. It was also that Keith was a fanatic about realism. If anything death-defying needed to be done for one of his parts, he wanted to do it. Carl always had the devil's own time arguing him out of it.

He was doing his best this time.

Finally Keith played his final card. "It will be a better movie. I can do it. I need to do it." He faced Garrison squarely. "I'll take full responsibility."

Garrison beamed. "Well, in that case..."

Carl muttered, but Garrison was convinced.

Jill wasn't, Luke could tell. "Are you sure about this?" she asked, her gray eyes looked worriedly into Keith's.

"'Course I'm sure." He brushed her lips with his. "Piece o' cake," he added. He took the flotation vest and began to put it on beneath his buckskin shirt.

Luke watched for a moment, felt his fists clench, then deliberately loosened them. He turned to help Carl get the canoe ready, then waited while Carl saw that the last of the safety lines were rigged.

Jill left Keith and followed Carl. "Are you sure there are enough? Is he safe?"

"As safe as I can make him," Carl said grimly.

Keith laughed and came after her, then kissed her again. "Don't worry about me. I'm the bread and butter around here. They won't let me drown!"

"But—"

"It's all right, Jilly," he insisted. "Better me than Luke here." He slanted a grin in Luke's direction. "He was partying a little too much last night."

"I was not!"

"Besides—" Keith grinned "—don't you know, cowboys can't swim!"

"I can so," Luke retorted.

"Not like I can. Who was California all-state breast-stroke champ in high school?"

Luke managed a smile at that. "*Breast* stroke?" He waggled his eyebrows. "You never told me that had anything to do with swimming."

Keith laughed easily. "Hey, not in front of my lady." He touched Jill's cheek. "Relax, hon, I'll be fine. Besides, it'll be a dynamite shot, you'll see. And everybody will know that it's really me."

"They won't care."

"But I care."

Luke saw their gazes catch and lock.

Finally Jill tore her eyes away from Keith and found Luke's, her gaze beseeching. "Can't you stop him?"

Can't you stop him?

He'd asked himself that time and again.

Could he have?

He didn't know. Maybe—if he'd argued harder. Maybe if he had, he would have won. God knew he should have tried. The fact was, he hadn't.

He'd kept his mouth shut and let Keith do the gag himself.

He'd have done it, pounding headache and roiling stomach and all, if Keith hadn't stepped in.

It was his job. But Keith was right about one thing: he wasn't a great swimmer. Not anywhere near as good as Keith. But if he did it right, he knew he wouldn't have to swim. He only had to launch the canoe, escape from the Indians who were shooting arrows at him and navigate the white water until he was around the bend in the river, where Carl's men were standing by to fish him out.

But Keith had pulled rank. "I'm the boss, remember," he said, then grinned. "C'mon, Carl, let's do it!"

Luke helped finish rigging the safety lines, then tossed a neon-colored volleyball into the current half a dozen times so they could figure out the best angles. Then it was Keith's turn.

"Outta my way, man," Keith said. He winked at Jill and headed up the draw, leaving Luke standing beside her on the riverbank. She glanced at Luke, then turned her gaze back to the river.

So did Luke. He edged away.

The scene went like clockwork—Keith's mad scramble down the draw, shoving off the canoe and leaping into it, his desperate paddling as the Indians swarmed after him, only to halt at the river's edge as the canoe shot away into the surging water, past the first set of rocks, over the rapids, downriver.

And then, suddenly, the canoe slewed sideways against the rocks. It plunged, tipped and flipped Keith into the water.

"*Keith!*" Jill swallowed her scream, pressing her hand to her mouth, watching frantically, waiting for him to surface. And when he didn't immediately, she turned to Luke, horrified, looking to him for help.

Luke shook his head and took a step back. "He'll be fine," he said gruffly. "He's got a vest. He'll be up in a sec. Just got to get his bearings."

This was Keith, after all. Keith, the all-state swimmer. Keith the champ. Keith who could do damn near everything Luke could do in the way of stunts—and when it came to water, could do them better. He was only showing off, trying to prove that it was a good thing he was doing it, not Luke.

"Don't worry," he said to Jill.

But when seconds turned into a minute, then two, and there was still no sign of Keith's dark head, his own determined calm disintegrated. Panic bubbled up.

He started toward the river, first walking, then running, then wading frantically out into the water, with Jill stumbling along behind him.

"Keith! Damn it, Keith!" He stumbled through the water, lost his footing, fell, scrambled up again. "Keith!"

Then Carl was beside him, too, looking feverishly around, muttering. "Damn him. If this is a joke..."

Luke knew what he meant. It wouldn't have been beyond him. He looked up onto the shore, hoping now that it was. Hoping to see Keith, irrepressible as ever, sitting on a rock laughing at them.

He saw instead Jill's white, stricken face. He turned back to the river and plunged in.

He didn't find Keith.

Carl didn't find Keith.

Neither did the grip downstream who pulled out the canoe half an hour later. Nor any of the hundreds of searchers who scoured the river for the rest of the day and evening.

They didn't find his body until the following morning, a mile downriver.

Luke had to go and identify him.

"We know who it is," the coroner apologized. "It's just a technicality."

It wasn't a technicality to Luke, not when he had to stand there and stare down into the dark, still, silent face of his friend. His ears rang. His throat closed. He felt himself start to shake.

"One of his boots was badly scraped," the coroner was saying matter-of-factly as he consulted the report. "We figure that's what held him down. It must have got stuck between two submerged rocks and he couldn't get out."

Luke wasn't looking at the boot. He was looking at the bloody, raw tips of Keith's fingers—mute testimony to his friend's desperate, futile struggle to free himself.

But if seeing Keith was hard, being the one to tell Jillian what she already knew was worse.

And worst of all was hearing from her lips what he already knew himself.

She didn't say anything for a moment, just stared into the distance. And then, in a low, toneless voice, she spoke. "He was doing your job," she said, and her gaze shifted so that she looked squarely at him, her eyes brimming with pain and unshed tears. "You were supposed to be out there, not him."

She wasn't telling him anything he hadn't already told himself. And all the guilt he'd had over the feelings he'd tried so long to hide was nothing compared to this.

No, they hadn't spoken at Keith's funeral.

What else had there been to say?

What was there to say now? Luke wondered as he rode slowly down toward his camp.

He tugged off his hat and raked a hand through damp hair, trying to muster what strength he had left. God knew he'd need it.

She was every bit as beautiful and as desirable as she'd ever been. And she had every right to hate his guts.

He rode up almost to where she stood, but he didn't dismount. It wasn't polite not to. He knew that. He also knew he needed every advantage he could get. "Jillian." His voice sounded rusty to his ears.

She looked up at him, and he feared for a moment that she might manage a smile. He was grateful when her lips stopped short of it.

"Luke."

He swallowed, waiting, expecting her to say why she'd come, but she didn't. She just looked at him. He felt like pond scum. Like cow dung. So he did what he'd always done when he'd been around her before—he resorted to sarcasm.

"Don't tell me," he said gruffly, "you were in the neighborhood."

Then he turned his horse and swung off, managing to keep his back to her the whole time. He walked his horse toward the pasture where he kept his mounts, hoping against hope that she would somehow vanish if he pretended she wasn't there.

She followed him. "I've been looking for you."

He didn't ask why. Instead he got a comb out of the saddlebag, loosened the cinch from his horse, then eased off the saddle and put it over the fence. He moved with the same focused deliberation he used when he was trying to forget the dream. The same deliberation he used to remind himself that this woman was off-limits. He laid the saddle blanket over the saddle, then took off the bridle, put on a halter and began to brush down his horse.

Jill was so close he could almost feel the heat of her breath against his sweat-soaked shirt. He inched away.

"You haven't been exactly easy to find."

"Didn't intend to be." He didn't look at her. He kept currying the horse, as if he did it every night. He reckoned the animal must be amazed at the attention.

"No one knew where you went."

"Somebody did," he pointed out. "You're here."

"A last shot. And it was pure luck."

"Is that what it is?" he said bitterly.

"I think so." Her voice was quiet.

"How were you so lucky?" He twisted the word. He couldn't help it.

"I decided to come back to where you and Keith met in the first place. And, well, I ran into a friend of yours."

Luke had thought his friends would have known better than to betray his whereabouts. "Who?"

"Paco."

Luke smothered a groan. "I might've known."

"He's a lovely little boy," Jill said quickly, defensively almost.

"He makes Machiavelli look like Little Bo-Peep."

She ventured a laugh and tossed a lock of hair away from her face. "He's delightful. A regular charmer." She was smiling, but as Luke turned, her smile faded. "He knows every movie Keith ever made."

His jaw tightened. "I know." He brushed past her and opened the gate so the horse could go into the pasture. Then he replaced the rungs of the gate before he turned back to ask roughly, "So, why were you looking? What do you want?"

"To... apologize."

"*Apologize?*" He stared at her, dumbfounded.

She nodded. "Apologize," she repeated firmly. "For what I said to you—to you...that day. The day I...the day you—"

"I know which day!" Did she think he'd ever forget?

"And I know I just made it worse for you. I wanted to say I'm sorry. I was...overwrought."

"You were right."

"No."

He jammed his hands into his pockets and stared out into the distance. "Yes. If I'd been doing my job, Keith wouldn't be dead."

"Keith liked to do his own stunts. It was his choice."

"That's no excuse. I should've told him—"

"Telling Keith never did any good at all, and you know it. Keith could talk his way around anyone. Even you," she added, giving him a level look. "You'd have had to knock him down and tie him up to have kept him out of that canoe."

"Then I should have," Luke said stubbornly. He kicked at the dirt with the toe of his scuffed boot. "Look," he said finally, "It was nice of you to drop by and apologize...." He still couldn't quite say the word with equanimity. "I appreciate it. Now it's gettin' late. It's gonna be dark before long and if you're gonna get down to the road before nightfall, you'd better get movin'."

"Luke—"

But he didn't want to hear any more. *Couldn't* listen to any more. He and Jillian Crane had never talked to each other. They didn't need to start now.

"Come on. I'll see you down." He whistled at the horses and they trotted his way, the bay gelding eagerly nosing his shirt pocket for the sugar he knew Luke kept there.

Aware that she was watching, he frowned and pushed the bay's head away, got nosed again and finally gave in and fed him a sugar cube. Then he slipped the halter over his head and led him out of the pasture.

"Shut the gate," he said over his shoulder and moved to saddle the horse.

She did. "Am I forgiven?"

He kept moving. "Of course."

"I didn't mean to hurt you. I—"

Luke wheeled around. "Look, what you said, I deserved. If you want me to forgive you, fine. You're forgiven. But it doesn't change a damn thing!"

"Because you haven't forgiven yourself," she said quietly.

"No, I haven't. You're right about that." His hands clenched against the saddle. He bent his head. He would never be able to forgive himself as long as he lived.

"You ought to, Luke," she said gently.

"I don't think so."

"Yes, you should. And you should stop hiding out up here and—"

"I'm not hiding out!"

"No one knew where you were."

"Paco did, obviously. So do most of the people in town."

"But they wouldn't tell me. Did you ask them not to?"

He shrugged irritably. "Didn't want to be bothered. Not that I reckon a lot of people would want to know," he added gruffly.

"I did. Carl would."

"No." Next to Jill, the last person he wanted to see was Carl, the man who had hired Luke in the first place and who had come to be the closest thing to a father Luke had

had in years. He'd done a lot of growing up under Carl's watchful, yet tolerant eye.

He didn't want to see the look in Carl's eyes now.

"Really, Luke—"

"No! And you'd damned well better not tell him where I am. Now come on. It's gettin' dark. You don't want to be trekking down the mountain in the dark."

"I could stay."

"The hell you could!" He looked at her, furious.

"We shared a house ... before."

Luke's jaw tightened and his fury grew as he remembered those two weekends when Keith had sent him with Jill up to his house in Big Bear in the hopes that the paparazzi would follow them and give him some space.

"A little bit of obscurity, privacy, heaven," Keith had said when he'd asked Luke to do it.

Heaven, yes. But in its own way, hell, too. Luke remembered only too well what had happened the last time they were there—those few brief moments when desire had defeated him, when he'd forgotten who she was, who he was, how wrong anything between them would be.

Anger and guilt swamped him even now. "Is that what this is all about? You looking to pick up where we left off, maybe? Are you horny, honey?"

She slapped his face.

They stared at each other. Then Luke raised a hand to touch his stinging cheek, while she pressed her fingers against her mouth and looked at him, stricken. "I'm sorry," she whispered.

He turned away. "You shouldn't be. You should have done it then."

And he strode quickly down to where she'd left her horse. It was Jimmy Kline's sorrel. He wondered how she'd managed that. But then Jillian had always had a way about her, a way that had made most of the world fall at her feet—especially, he thought savagely, grown men who should damn well have known better.

"How'd you get Kline's horse?" he demanded.

"Paco introduced us. They were a little less eager to let me know where you were," she admitted. "But Paco convinced them."

"I'll bet," he said grimly. Well, the deed was done. Now he just wanted her gone. "At least you knew enough to loosen the cinch," he grunted.

"Jimmy told me to."

"Good ol' Jimmy," he said under his breath. He turned to her. "Get on." He swung easily into the bay's saddle. "Let's go." He started down the trail without looking back, wanting to get far enough ahead so they wouldn't have to talk.

But Jill caught up with him. "I didn't just come to apologize. And I didn't come for what else you implied," she said flatly. "I came because I need your help. I'm working on a book. A biography. Of Keith."

He didn't even look at her. He just kept riding, giving no sign that he'd even heard, wishing he hadn't. It didn't stop her.

"I've been working on it for the past year," she continued. "I've got almost all the interviewing done. I've talked to everyone who ever meant anything to Keith. Teachers, friends, relatives, directors, producers, other actors. Everyone, that is, except..." She didn't have to finish.

"No." *God, no.*

"I know you think it would be painful to talk about it," she said urgently. "All right, it *is* painful. But it also helps, Luke, believe me." She urged the sorrel forward until she rode beside him. "I didn't want to do it, either. But it gave me some perspective."

"I've got all the perspective I need." It was over. Past. And he couldn't talk about it. Couldn't relive it. Especially not with her. He'd never survive.

He urged his horse on, trotting now, keeping far enough ahead of her all the way down the road so that she would have had to shout for him to hear. Finally they reached the next gate. "Just follow the trail on down. Another half mile and you'll see the ranch house. You're almost there." He turned his horse.

"Luke, listen—"

"No. Goodbye, Jill." His voice was hard and flat. He didn't look back.

Two

Hell, Luke thought as he flung himself onto his narrow cot. Who needed dreams to wake him quivering and shaking? Who needed dreams to make him ache?

Not him. Hell, no.

Tonight he had reality to do the trick.

All the damned work he'd done all day, all the wood he'd chopped when he'd got back up the mountain, all the shirts he scrubbed threadbare on the old washboard well into the night hadn't banished reality one bit.

He only had to turn his head to see out the window to the tree where she'd tied her horse. Even in the shadowy moonlight, he only had to glance toward the pasture. He could see the stump where she'd stood. He only had to shut his eyes and in his mind he could see his cabin. But now when he saw the front steps, she was standing there.

Jillian.

Jillian Crane.

God, he thought as he stared up at the rough-hewn ceiling, why Jill? Of all the women in the world, why her?

For almost two years he hadn't seen her. He'd figured he wouldn't have to see her ever again. He'd counted it one of his very few blessings.

And now, out of the blue, she was here. Right here. On his mountain.

Standing mere inches from him. So close he could have touched her. So close her breath had actually touched him.

Damn it to hell.

And she'd come to apologize to him!

Apologize! When God knew he ought to have been on his knees apologizing to her.

Instead he'd done his best to insult her, to remind her of the one thing he should have pretended to forget—the day he had kissed her.

The day he'd discovered that, for all that she was his best friend's fiancée, he didn't have the self-control he ought to have. For a few brief moments he'd taken her for himself!

He'd had no right.

She was Keith's from the start. Luke hadn't even been around when Keith met her. He'd broken his leg during a chase scene toward the end of the filming of *Tiger's Dreams,* a movie they were working on in Spain. And as soon as he was able, Luke had flown back to California to recuperate.

Keith had gone on to London with the rest of the crew to finish up some interiors in the studio there. Near the end of filming, two days before he was due to come home, an American magazine writer named Jillian Crane had gone to London to interview him for an in-depth profile.

Luke never knew exactly what had happened at that interview. It was enough that Keith hadn't come back to California with the rest of the crew. Instead he'd flown to the Caribbean for "a little R and R" and a lot more in-depth discussion with Jillian Crane.

When he finally did come back to Los Angeles three weeks later, the article was finished; Jill wasn't.

She and Keith were a pair.

The first time Luke saw her was the day she and Keith had got back to L.A. He'd been staying at Keith's house because his own apartment had too many steps for a man just getting used to his walking cast.

He'd been limping around the kidney-shaped pool, when suddenly Keith had appeared in the doorway.

"Hey, Luke! You can walk again! So, c'mere. Want you to meet my lady."

"Your... lady?" He had never heard Keith call any woman that before. He glanced up, curious, to see a serious, dark-haired beauty looking at him. His heart skipped a beat. He took a step, slipped in a puddle and landed on his rear end.

They both rushed to his aid. Keith was laughing and grumbling. "Knocked you right on your can, did she? I'm not surprised."

"Are you all right?" the woman asked. She was leaning over him, patting him, her dark hair tickling against his bare chest.

"I'm fine," Luke snapped, brushing them both off, mortified by his clumsiness, which was a direct result of his instant reaction to Keith's "lady."

He still was mortified every time he remembered what had happened that day. But in retrospect, he supposed his falling was the best thing that could have happened. It had prompted him to shove Jill away then. And that had set the tone of his relationship with her ever since.

She was Keith's lady, so Luke steered as clear of her as he could. It wasn't easy. Keith didn't drop his friends when he found a woman. Instead, he tried to get everyone together. For Luke it didn't work. He told himself that she had no affect on him or on his life at all. It wasn't true, of course. He couldn't look at her without feeling a renewed surge of attraction. And it didn't take long to figure out that the attraction was more than physical. He liked Jill Crane.

He liked the way she listened when people talked, liked her no-nonsense approach to Keith's very crazy, fast-lane life. He told himself she was stodgy, that after Jill's advent into his life, Keith changed. He became quieter, more introspective.

"Sane," Carl had said, laughing.

Probably. There had never been anything very sane about the things Luke and Keith did together. They went skydiving, shark hunting, motorcycle racing, and did a dozen other things, each more crazy and daring than the last. They were stubborn, competitive and tough as nails.

"Tryers," Keith called them. "Two of a kind."

But Jill brought out a side of Keith Luke really didn't know.

"A kinder, gentler Keith," Luke remembered scoffing when Keith had declined to go out bar hopping with him and another friend one night. "Man, has she got you tied down."

But Keith had just grinned and tugged Jill into his lap, shrugging equably. "Eat your heart out, chum," was all he'd said.

He never knew that there were times when Luke had. Luke had put up a good front. He'd told himself, Keith—

hell, the whole world—that he didn't need sweetness and light and a gentle woman like Jill. As for the gentler side of himself, he wasn't sure he had one.

It was a damn sight easier to tell himself that if he wanted to steer clear of her.

And he did. He had . . . until that last afternoon at Big Bear.

They'd spent the weekend together, just he and Jill. It had been all Keith's fault, but he wanted a little time "out of the fishbowl," as he called it. It had worked once before when Luke had decoyed the press away, pretending to be Keith. He'd hated doing it, but he could understand why Keith asked him to. Fame wasn't always easy, and Keith went out of his way for his fans almost every day. He needed a little break.

So when Keith asked, Luke had gone. He'd argued that he could decoy them alone, but Keith had disagreed.

"You have to take Jill. If she isn't there, they won't believe you're me."

And so the two of them went together. Jill did her best to be pleasant and cheerful and polite. Luke did his best to be surly and uncommunicative. He didn't really want to be, but it seemed the smartest—and safest—way to spend a weekend with her.

But spending forty-eight hours in her company was an exercise in frustration beyond belief. Not only because he found her physically attractive, but because she was a nice person, a caring person. If he let her, she'd bring out the same good qualities in him that she brought out in Keith. Luke didn't dare. Because if he did, she'd bring out something else, too.

Finally, late Sunday afternoon, as they were lying beside the pool, he decided he just might make it through. There were only a few more hours to endure, when Jill glanced up from her book and said, "Don't look now, but there's a photographer trying to get a shot over the fence. Probably looking for a real hot picture." She grinned conspiratorially at Luke, then blew him a kiss.

A weekend's worth of frustration boiled over.

"Then let's give him something to really look at," he growled. And before he had time for second thoughts, he swung himself over by her chaise longue and kissed her hard on the mouth.

He'd meant it as a gesture. Nothing more, nothing less.

The photographer wanted to see some hot stuff? Well, fine, Luke would show him!

But he was the one who'd been shown.

He and, he supposed, Jill.

He touched his lips to hers, and what began as a kiss ended as a conflagration. Searing in intensity, burning in desperation. Mad and crazy and foolhardy, it endured and deepened, and finally shook him to the depths of his soul.

God knew where it would have ended if Jill hadn't finally pulled back, pressing her hand against her mouth and looking up at him with wide, frightened eyes.

"Keith," she whispered, horrified.

Luke's jaw locked. An eternity passed. Then he muttered an expletive under his breath and dove into the blessedly cold water of the pool. But he'd never been able to wash away the guilt.

She was back.

Luke couldn't believe it.

He'd spent the entire day doing his best to blot out the memory of Jillian Crane sitting on his doorstep just the night before, and he came over the rise that evening and damned if she wasn't sitting there again.

His horse, sensing sudden tension in the hand that held the reins, tossed his head and sidestepped.

"It's all right," Luke said automatically, reaching out to pat the horse's neck.

But it wasn't. It wasn't all right at all.

She'd seen him and was getting to her feet. She lifted a hand, but then dropped it and stood waiting, feet slightly apart. She looked like Annie Oakley ready to take on the bad guys at high noon.

And he was definitely one of the bad guys.

He should have realized that brushing her off yesterday had been too easy. This was Jill Crane he was dealing with. She might have been Keith's fiancée, but she was still a competent, diligent professional writer, an award-winning personality profiler.

He knew she didn't leave any stone unturned when it came to getting her story. Jill went after people like one of those old-time sheriffs who always got his man.

But she damned well wasn't getting him.

Nothing said he had to talk to her. And nothing on earth would get him to.

Once—*once*—he'd succumbed to her in a moment of weakness. It wasn't happening again.

As far as Jillian Crane and Lucas Tanner were concerned, *nothing* was happening again.

It was hard enough to live with the past if he just managed to leave it there. He was damned if he was going to rake it all up again. Least of all with her.

He scowled fiercely at her as he rode in.

"Well, here I am again," she said in a singsong, self-mocking tone.

"Why?"

"You know why. The book. It's important—to me, to Carl, to Keith's friends and to his fans. And whether ei-

her of us likes it or not, Luke, you're part of it. So—"
he shrugged "—I guess I hoped you'd thought about it
and changed your mind."

"All the thinking in the world isn't going to change my
mind. I told you. No."

And he'd keep saying no until kingdom come if that's
what it took. He swung down out of the saddle and faced
her head-on. "Believe it. There's nothing you can do or
say that will make any difference."

"You owe it to Keith."

It was like a knife in the heart.

He'd thought that nothing could touch him, that he
was impervious, that he was prepared for any argument,
could turn his back on any plea.

He wasn't prepared for that.

He swallowed a curse. He turned away, his fury making his fingers fumble as he tried to loosen the cinch.
"Damn you. Keith wouldn't have asked that."

"Probably not. But then, Keith's not here to ask it, is
he?"

God, it wasn't enough that she thrust the knife in. Now
she had to twist it.

He spun around. "Damn it! How low are you gonna
go?"

She winced and paled, but stood her ground, looking
at him defiantly. "As low as I have to, I guess."

All the four-letter words he could think of tumbled
around in his head. He yanked the saddle off, opened the
gate and slapped the horse's rump so that it trotted into
the pasture.

"Is this your revenge?" he asked finally.

"Revenge?" She frowned briefly, then shook her head.
"Believe it or not, Luke, I'm not trying to hurt you."

He snorted. No, he didn't believe it. Why should he?

She had a right to revenge, even if he wouldn't have expected it of her. But then, up until their kiss, he'd never given her much credit for passion, either.

Obviously Lucas Tanner had a lot to learn about women.

Would Keith have wanted him to cooperate?

Probably, he admitted. Keith was a star, eager for recognition. He relished the limelight.

He'd have preferred to have the limelight and a good long life, of course. But going out in the spectacular way he had would have appealed to his sense of drama. Afterward, though, he would want a good accounting.

Jill would give him a good accounting.

"You got all those other people. You don't need me," Luke argued.

"You were closer to him than anyone else. You were his best friend."

"Some friend," Luke muttered. He sighed and rubbed the back of his neck. "What do I have to do?"

"Talk to me about how you two met. Tell me about your relationship, the good things and the bad, what Keith meant to you."

"Nothing much, huh?" he said ironically.

"I know it will be hard. But there were good times, Luke. A lot of them." She looked at him beseechingly. "It's a chance to remember them."

"That's supposed to make me feel better? How about thinking about all the good times we could have had if I'd done my job?" He spun away from her and started walking toward the cabin, the saddle in his arms.

She came after him. "I told you, it wasn't your fault. But we can talk about that, too, if you want."

He spun around and glowered at her. "I damned well do not want!"

She took a step back, then said quietly, "It might help."

"Let's get one thing straight right off. If I talk to you for your book, I'm talkin' just for your book. I'm not talkin' to ease my pain."

"Because you want to wallow in it?"

"Go to hell!" He started to turn away again.

"I've been there," she said quietly.

They stared at each other. All the pain, all the memories, everything he never wanted to think about again hung there between them.

Luke dragged a palm down his face. "How long will it take?"

"It depends."

"On what?"

"On you. On how much you're willing to tell me and how long it takes you to get to it."

He started walking again. "I'm not willing to tell you anything and you know it."

"Then on how well you cooperate unwillingly." She was walking alongside him, and the wind carried the scent of something faintly flowery that he knew would be haunting him tonight.

He put the saddle in the shed, then headed toward the cabin. But when he got there, he didn't open the door. He stopped on the narrow front porch and folded his arms across his chest. He wasn't inviting her in. She'd invaded his mountain. She wasn't invading his home.

"So ask," he said.

She blinked. "Not tonight. I don't want to just get started and have to stop. I'll come back tomorrow."

"No."

She looked taken aback.

"I'm workin' tomorrow," he explained, moderating his tone.

"I'll come along."

"No!" She much for moderation.

"It would be easiest. I—"

"I said no. You want me to talk, I'll talk. But you aren't going to follow me around."

"Then I'll be here when you get back tomorrow night."

"No. I'll come down. I'll meet you at the Klines' after I finish up here."

"It will be almost dark. You said—"

"I'll meet you at the Klines'. Tomorrow night. Take it or leave it." *Leave it,* he prayed. *Leave it.*

Jill met his gaze, then nodded. "The Klines'," she agreed.

He ground his teeth. "Be there by seven."

"I'm staying there."

"What?" How the hell had she wangled that? Did she know the house was his, that Jimmy and Annette were just renting it?

"Paco arranged it."

"That manipulating little son of a—"

"You like him."

"Like I like poison ivy," Luke grumbled.

Jill shook her head. She was smiling slightly. "He showed me the Porsche you carved for him. And the animals."

"Hell." The kid had no sense, no sense at all. Luke had figured the boy might show his mother the half-dozen wooden toys he'd made him. He didn't expect him to show the whole damn world. He let out an explosive breath. "Is there anything he didn't show you? Or tell you?"

"I don't know," Jill said gravely. "I'll ask him."

Luke muttered under his breath, then jammed his hands into his pockets. "I don't know what time I'll finish. I'll be down when I get done."

"I'll make us dinner."

"I'll eat on the way down. Go on now, or it'll be dark." He turned and stalked toward where she'd left the horse. He untied the reins and slapped them into her hand.

"Is this a hint, Lucas?"

He scowled. "What do you think?"

She stood there with the reins in her hand, then she looked at him. He held himself still and met her gaze. But it seemed to take forever until she was finally in the saddle again.

"I'll see you tomorrow then," she said quietly.

He wished to God he could say, *Not if I see you first.*

Luke reckoned that being stuck in a blizzard might be excuse enough not to have to go down the mountain the following night. Or being eaten by a swarm of deerflies. Or dying in a forest fire. Or getting mauled by a bear.

Naturally, he wasn't so lucky. He survived the day intact, the weather turned warm, almost balmy, and the sky was a cloudless blue when he got back to the cabin shortly before six.

He took his own sweet time washing off in the creek, but finally he had no choice. He had to put on a clean shirt, comb his hair, slap his hat on his head, saddle a fresh horse and make his way down to the ranch house.

He might not know Jillian well, but he knew her well enough to be sure that she'd come after him if he didn't.

And while he was there he had a few things to say to Jimmy. There was no point in talking to Annette.

She'd had a crush on him since she was seven. He reckoned it was his good fortune—and hers—that she'd outgrown it enough so that when Jimmy Kline got old enough to ask her to marry him, she agreed instead of waiting for Luke.

She'd have waited forever before he got around to asking; probably she knew it.

When he reached the ranch house, he found Jimmy in the barn. The younger man looked up and grinned nervously. "You ain't mad, are you?"

"Whatever gave you that idea?" Luke's studied mildness made Jimmy wince.

He raked a hand through his thatch of red hair. "I told Annette we didn't have no business lettin' Jill stay here. I said it was up to you, it bein' your ranch an' all. But she'd already told Jill she could 'cause she was a friend of yours. Figured you'd be glad, she said. I guess you ain't." He'd figured out that much, at least.

Luke shrugged. He could think of several pithy things to say, all of which would be in vain. Jimmy understood—or thought he did. And Annette never would.

"Don't matter," he said now.

"It ain't entirely Annette's fault," Jimmy confessed after a moment. "I kinda liked the idea of havin' her here right now, too. Y'know, Annette's gettin' pretty big. She's due this month. And she was almost a month early when she had Jimmy."

Luke hadn't been there when eighteen-month-old Jimmy, Jr. was born, so he didn't remember that. But he could attest to the truth of Jimmy's earlier statement. Last time he'd seen Annette, she'd looked like a barn moving sideways.

It would be better to have someone on hand to take her to the hospital, in case Annette went into labor while

Jimmy was out on the range. Even if that someone was Jill Crane.

"I see what you mean," he said.

Jimmy looked enormously relieved. "I'll take care of your horse," he offered.

"Jill in the house?"

"Ready and waitin'. We'll keep outta your way."

Luke would have rather had them in his way, but he didn't say so. He left the horse for Jimmy to deal with and headed toward the house.

Annette had the door open the minute his boot hit the first step. "Luke!" She practically grabbed his arm to draw him in. "You came! I was really scared you'd be mad at me 'cause you're so—so kind of touchy... about... well, you know what about. But I guess you really want to talk to Jill, huh?"

Under the barrage of her enthusiasm, Luke didn't reply. Over Annette's shoulder he saw Jill sitting on the sofa, giving Jimmy, Jr. a bottle. She looked up when he came into the room. "He's almost asleep. I'm sorry. Do you mind waiting?"

He shook his head, mute, his gaze caught by the sight of her with the baby in her arms. He'd never thought about Jill with children before. She looked right at home. He jerked his hat off and crushed the brim in his fingers.

"Sit down," Annette said. "Sit down." Then she giggled and put her hand over her mouth. "Gosh, I'm dumb, tellin' you to sit down in your own house."

A tiny frown appeared on Jill's face, and he guessed that answered his question about whether or not she knew who owned the ranch. Well, if it made her uncomfortable, too bad. He hadn't invited her, and maybe she'd leave all that much sooner.

He said nothing, just sat down, balancing the hat on his thighs.

Annette waddled between him and Jill. "Can I bring you some coffee? And brownies? I made brownies today. And I got some butterscotch bars left, too. I made those Tuesday. Would you rather have those?"

"No, thanks. I ate on the way down."

"Oh, but—"

"I'm fine," he said firmly.

Jill stood up, smiling at the child in her arms, then looked over at Annette. "He's asleep," she said softly. "I'll just go put him in his crib."

"I don't know what I'd be doin' without her," Annette said to Luke as Jill carried the small, limp body of her son up the stairs to the bedroom. "I can't hardly carry him anymore 'cause of this watermelon here." She giggled and patted her stomach. "Jill's doin' everything."

Luke nodded absently. He wasn't looking at Annette's stomach; he was looking at the stairs. Though Jill had already disappeared into the bedroom, he could still see her as she'd looked carrying the little boy up them. She'd looked so natural. Hell, she'd have probably had one of her own by now, if only...

He let out a harsh exhalation of breath.

"Somethin' the matter?" Annette asked worriedly.

Luke shook his head. But he was almost grateful when, a moment later, Jill returned. She was carrying with her a loose-leaf notebook, a pen and a small tape recorder. "Where do you want to work?"

Luke glanced at Annette.

"I'll be quiet as a mouse," she promised.

Jill smiled at the younger woman. "I don't think that will work very well," she said apologetically. "Having someone listening tends to make the person I'm talking with uncomfortable.''

"Not me," Luke said. No matter what Annette said about being quiet, he knew it was impossible. And the more she talked, the less he'd have to.

"And it makes me a little uncomfortable, too," Jill went on smoothly. "So I think we'll go for a walk."

"Oh," Annette said, crestfallen.

"Oh," said Luke. Hell.

Jill pulled on a sweater and went to the door, then looked back at him. Reluctantly, he followed her.

"Maybe you'll have a brownie when you get back?" Annette called after him.

Luke grunted a noncommittal response and shut the door.

"She's very fond of you," Jill said as they stepped off the porch.

"She used to be my sister-in-law."

Jill gaped. She dropped her pen and had to scramble for it. He reached down to get it for her and nearly bumped heads with her.

"I didn't realize you were ever . . . married," she said.

"I wasn't. My older brother was married to her sister when they were little more than kids. It didn't work out," he added after a moment.

Another disaster that could be laid at his door. If he hadn't been such a damned hothead after his old man died, lashing out at an unfair world and carrying a chip the size of the whole damned state of Colorado on his shoulder, always getting into trouble and expecting his brother to bail him out, Tanner might have been home the night that Clare had needed him, the night their son was born—and died.

He sighed and tugged his hat down.

"I'm sorry," Jill said gently.

Luke shrugged. "They're both doin' all right now."

That was his only consolation—knowing that, though the youthful marriage had collapsed after less than a year, Clare had now been happily married for nearly twelve years to a local doctor, and Tanner had finally met and married the right woman for him.

Luke didn't know much about his new sister-in-law, Maggie, but she sure seemed to have made a difference in his brother's life.

"Old Sobersides," Luke had called his older brother, Robert, whom all the world but Maggie called Tanner. And the Old Sobersides appellation had come only if Luke was feeling charitable.

Usually he'd just called Tanner "The Grouch."

But Tanner wasn't grouchy these days. Ever since the wedding, he'd been smiling. And his smile had been especially broad in the last photo Maggie had sent Luke— one in which Tanner was holding their new son, Jared.

And damned if that thought didn't bring him right back to babies.

"Let's get on with this," he said harshly. "I haven't got all night."

"Is there a place we can go and sit down so I can write, or do you want me to tape while we walk and talk?"

Luke shrugged. "Doesn't matter. You're the biographer, not me." But he was shifting from one foot to the other as he said it, and apparently Jill noticed.

"We'll tape," she said. "And walk." She left the notebook sitting by the gate and turned on the tape recorder. It was tiny enough that she could hold it in her palm.

Luke looked at it warily. "That what you used on Keith?"

"A similar one, yes. But I took notes, too, because we were just sitting talking."

"For *three weeks?*"

She flushed. "At the interview. The three weeks was vacation."

"Right. I forgot."

Damn, what was he doing? He didn't care what they'd been doing down in the Caribbean. It wasn't any of his business. He needed to get out of here before he said something else stupid. "First question?" he prompted.

"Why don't you tell me about how you two met."

"That isn't a question."

"It's a request."

"You know all that," he protested.

"Not really. I know you were a cowboy around here and he met you when he was doing a movie. I don't know exactly how it happened."

No, probably she didn't. There was no reason why Keith would have told her. It hadn't changed anything much—at the time, anyway—for Keith.

It had changed Luke's whole life.

"I was workin' at Mike Sutter's spread across the valley," he said reluctantly, "and Keith's bunch was there making *Renegade's Moon*."

"So it was almost seven years ago?"

"Yeah. They were shooting a scene, and one of their cameramen was wavin' his arms around, and he spooked some cattle. I headed 'em off and turned 'em before they ran the damn fool down."

"He must have been grateful."

"I guess. Babbled all over me. Heck, what was I supposed to do, let 'em trample him? It turned out Carl was watching and he needed somebody to do the same thing in the movie. So he asked me."

"And that's when you were hired?"

Luke shook his head. "I told him I already had a job."

He could still remember Carl looking at him dumb-founded when he'd said that. "He sorta drew himself up and tried to loom over me, asking, 'And you'd rather herd cows than work in the movies?' I said, 'Well, it's my job. I can't just leave my boss in the lurch,' and he said, 'And who is this boss who inspires such undying loyalty?' So I told him, and he went to Mike and told him to fire me."

"You're kidding."

"Nope. You know Carl. He doesn't believe in no. Mike said the hell he would. But then Carl explained what he wanted and Mike said it was all right with him, so I did it."

"Were you scared?"

"I didn't know what to expect. Turned out it wasn't any big deal, really. Hell, I did it damn near every day of the week. But afterward they were all runnin' around, slappin' me on the back and saying, 'You're some horse-backin' fool! Man, how'd you learn to do that?'"

"How did you?"

Luke shrugged. "Grew up doin' it. My old man was a cowboy. My brothers are cowboys."

"I don't know anything about your family," Jill said, considering him thoughtfully. "Do you realize you've never even mentioned them to me? Do your brothers work around here?"

"No." He didn't want to talk about them, or about anything else that was personal. "I thought we were talkin' about Keith."

"And we can't discuss anything else?"

"I didn't come down here to talk about anything else."

She gave a small snort of impatience, then shrugged. "Fine. So, you had your one day of glory. Did you meet Keith then?"

"Nope. Did that the next day. Carl asked me to come back. He wondered if I could fall off."

"He wanted you to fall off a horse?"

Luke nodded. "He said, 'We'll pay you $400.' I thought he was nuts. *'Four hundred dollars?'* I said. Hell, first time anybody ever offered to pay me for what I'd been doin' for nothin' for years!" He couldn't help grinning at the memory of his own astonishment.

"So I said sure, why not? Next day, when I showed up, Brent Hubbard—you know Brent, one of the stuntmen?" He looked at her and when she nodded, he continued, "Well, he asked me if I wanted some pads. I didn't know what he meant. 'Pads?' I asked him, 'What for?' 'Hip, knee, wrist, elbow, tailbone,' he said, and looked at me like I ought to know what he was talking about. But I didn't, and when I just stared at him, he told me to take down my pants."

Jill's eyes widened, and Luke flushed, realizing that she'd think he was an idiot for sure if he told her what he'd thought at first when Brent had said that!

"Anyway," he hurried on, "I found out what pads were when they put 'em on me. And I wore 'em while I did the riding and the falling. I was done before noon and I figured I'd better get movin' or Mike was gonna think I'd gone and quit on him. But Carl called me over and that's when I met Keith."

He could remember it as clearly as if it were yesterday.

"I recognized him," Luke admitted, "but it was like meetin' somebody whose name you've forgotten. I was saying, 'Hey, how are ya?' like I knew him because his face was familiar, but I didn't have a clue who he was."

Jill smiled. "Did he know that?"

"Of course. Later, he used to tell me he'd rescued me from a life of cultural ignorance." Luke grinned at the memory, and Jill grinned, too.

"Anyhow," he said abruptly, turning his head away from that grin, "that's how I met Keith. Carl thought I resembled him, and he wanted Keith to see what he thought. He should've known better. Keith didn't care how much I looked like him or didn't. He just wanted me to teach him everything crazy I knew how to do."

"I'll bet he did," Jill said softly.

Their eyes met again, and hers had the same gentle, wistful expression that Luke remembered seeing sometimes when he'd caught her watching Keith. The same slightly dazed look he'd seen in them the moment he'd kissed her, before she'd realized what they were doing.

He jaw tightened. He jerked his eyes away and started walking again rapidly. "I did his stunt work for the rest of the movie. Then he asked me to go back to California with him to work on his next one. And I figured, why the hell not? So I went."

"Was it a big change?"

He frowned. "From cowboying? Hell, yes. Cowboying, I did whatever needed to be done. Saw it and did it. Out there I always had somebody figurin' out what I was supposed to be doing. How fast I was supposed to be going. Which way to turn my head so's I'd look pretty for a camera. Or so's Keith would look pretty," he corrected. His gaze narrowed again at a sudden realization. "How come we're talkin' about me again, not Keith?"

"We're talking about both of you," Jill said patiently. "About the relationship between you. Relationships are complex."

"Not ours. It was simple. Keith Mallory was my friend. The best damn friend I ever had." He looked at her bleakly. "And I as good as killed him."

Jill's fingers clutched his arm hard through his thin cotton shirt. "Stop saying that. It isn't true."

"Isn't it?" He gave a harsh laugh. "Well, I guess that's debatable," he said bitterly, staring off into the distance. Then his gaze shifted and came back to meet hers. He swallowed. "But you can't tell me that once I—*we*—didn't betray him."

Three

―

"**I** know."

Luke didn't know what he'd been hoping. Maybe that she'd deny it, tell him he was wrong, that he'd been imagining things, thinking things that weren't true and never had been.

She didn't. She met his gaze squarely, her gray eyes dark now, yet oddly luminous and shining with moisture. Tears? Ah, God, no. He looked at her, anguished.

"You didn't want me to agree with you?" she asked him softly.

He kicked at a stone in the field. "No, damn it, I didn't."

"But it's true." She stared out across the valley. There was a small cluster of lights where Bluff Springs was and dotted across the far side of the valley were the isolated lights of ranch houses.

"It shouldn't have been," he said hollowly.

"No."

He toed a clump of grass this time. "You should've stopped me."

"Yes."

"Why didn't you?"

She shook her head. In the deepening twilight he could make out a tear as it trickled down her cheek. She didn't wipe it away. She just stared resolutely out across the valley. "I don't know," she said.

"You didn't even like me."

"I tried. When did you ever give me any reason to? From the day I showed up, you acted like I was contaminated or something."

"I never—"

"You were sarcastic and gruff, and every time I walked into the room, you left."

How could he explain what he'd felt from the first moment he'd seen her? How could he possibly tell her that just being around her made him feel awkward and unpolished, like the dumb, tongue-tied cowboy he was?

And the fact that Keith was clearly different when he was with her, calmer and more focused—a *gentleman,* for God's sake—didn't help matters, either.

"I never disliked you," he insisted. "I just— Hell, I kissed you, didn't I?"

"But why? Why did you?"

He stuffed his hands into his pockets and shrugged. "You were there."

"And Keith wasn't."

"No, that's not why, damn it! I wasn't doing it to try to beat out Keith!"

"Then why?"

He jerked off his hat and rubbed a hand through his hair, then shook his head. He couldn't begin to explain the combination of frustration and anger and hunger that had been building in him for so long. He knew better, damn it. He just—just . . .

"Because you were horny, honey?" she said lightly, mocking the words he'd said to her the day before.

Luke scowled and jammed his hat back on his head. "Yeah," he muttered. "I probably was."

"And I was handy."

His jaw tightened. He nodded curtly.

"Any woman would have done?"

"That's right." The look he gave her dared her to argue.

She didn't, and somehow that annoyed him even further.

"So, what was your excuse?" he demanded. "Why did you respond? You did, you know," he added, in case she wanted to deny it.

She didn't answer immediately. She seemed to be actually considering the question. Then she shook her head, a bewildered look on her face. "I'm not sure."

"You're not sure?" he said sarcastically.

"I don't know."

He turned away. "Well, when you figure it out, let me know."

"I will."

He shook his head. "You know, you are really a piece of work, lady."

"An observation not to be taken as a compliment?"

He turned and caught a wry smile on her mouth. That almost-smile did something to his insides, brought back the very same feeling that had welled up within him that afternoon when he had succumbed to frustration, to temptation—to her.

He jerked his gaze away, angry with himself. "Take it any way you like," he growled, kneading tight muscles in the back of his neck. "I can't do this," he said abruptly.

"Can't do what?"

"This. Talk. Soul search." He twisted the words as he said them.

"You brought it up."

"I shouldn't have."

"If it needed to be said—"

"It didn't."

"Fine, let's talk about Keith."

"No. I told you, I can't. If you really need me to, give me some tapes and your tape recorder. I'll tell what I know into the tapes."

"I have to ask—"

"Tapes," he insisted. "Tapes or nothing. Look," he argued when she didn't reply, "it'll be better for you. If I do tapes, you don't have to hang around here waiting. Leave your address with Annette. I'll bring 'em down when I'm done and she can mail them to you."

"How do I know you won't just head back up into the hills and forget you ever saw me?"

"I wish to God I could."

"Luke..."

"I'll do it," he promised her. "I owe it to Keith."

"I didn't mean—"

"No. You were right. And I'll pay what I owe. But, for God's sake, let me pay it my way."

She opened her mouth to speak again, but he forestalled her. "Please."

His fingers curled into fists. He stared resolutely out across the now-dark valley. He couldn't look at her. He knew what he'd see—that look of wide-eyed confusion

mingling with anticipation that he remembered all too
well. The look she'd had when he'd kissed her.

"I'll do tapes," he said again. It was his last offer.

Jill sighed. "All right."

Inarticulate didn't begin to describe him.

Tongue-tied would have been a compliment.

Why he had ever thought talking on tape would be
easy, Luke didn't know. It wasn't.

He started, stopped, mumbled, erased, cursed, muttered, started—and stopped—again. And again.

He'd practically flunked speech in high school. What
had he been thinking of, for Pete's sake?

He'd been thinking of avoiding Jill.

It was as simple as that. But in fact, he didn't seem to
be able to avoid her at all.

Oh, personally she might be back in New York, but in
his mind—his damned, irritating, contrary mind—she
was alive and well in those half-dozen little plastic cas-
settes that sat on his shelf and mocked him day after day,
night after night.

When he couldn't just sit down and mindlessly rattle
things off the way he'd hoped to, he thought if he prepared, then just spouted the words into the recorder, he
could get enough distance from the topic—and from the
woman—to do it.

So he spent his days when he was out checking the
cattle and riding fence thinking about what he wanted to
say, then scribbling notes in a pocket-size notebook.

But it didn't take him long to realize that writing down
notes just meant he spent all day, every day, thinking
about *not* thinking about her.

And thinking about Keith.

For almost two years he'd done his best not to think about either of them. With Keith it had simply been too painful at first. And with Jill...it had seemed far smarter not to.

He'd survived by focusing on the present, on this cow and that calf, on this fence and that piece of wire. He had managed to hang onto his sanity—just—by deliberately not thinking about the last seven years of his life.

But once he started to do what he'd told Jillian he would do, the memories just kept welling up, even though he couldn't seem to talk about them.

And with them came a whole roller coaster's worth of emotions. Ever since Keith's death Luke had been plagued by one in particular—guilt. But now, as he let his mind play back over the time he'd been Keith's friend, he found that there was a lot more to it. He was, by turns, sad and happy, angry and amused, delighted and distraught as he remembered the years he'd spent in the charmed world of Keith Mallory, God's gift to film, fans and friends.

And he found, oddly, that though he couldn't talk to the tape without feeling like a gold-plated fool, he had plenty to say to Keith.

"This is all your fault," Luke told his friend. He shoved himself further up against the tree trunk he was sitting in front of and rubbed Hank's back. Then he tossed a stone into the swift current of the river. "If you hadn't come up here making your damned movies, none of this would have happened."

It was midafternoon. The day was warm, working its way toward downright hot, and he'd spent the morning moving a couple bunches of cattle to new pasture. He had some more to move later, but cattle weren't fools. They moved easier when it was cooler, and Luke didn't mind waiting and shading up a bit while he ate a sandwich and drank some juice.

As he sat there with the dogs at his feet, he remembered the last time he'd sat under this tree. That afternoon almost two years ago, right before they'd started shooting up on the Salmon.

He and Keith had decided to take the long way around. It was the first time in over a year that they'd gone off, just the two of them, to raise a little hell and have a good time.

It had been Keith's idea; he'd suggested it right after the weekend Luke and Jill had spent at Big bear. Jill had left to do a series of interviews in the East, and Keith had found himself with time on his hands.

"Let's do it," he'd said. "I won't be able to once I'm an old married man." He'd given Luke a lascivious wink. "Not that I'll be complaining."

And Luke, who was doing his best to forget kissing Jill, hadn't quite been able to look Keith in the eye. But the notion of just the two of them roughnecking around sounded good. "Whatever you want," he'd said gruffly.

They'd set off without any particular aim other than to go somewhere they could hang out where no one would recognize Keith or, if they did, wouldn't bother him.

The only place Luke could think of was his old stomping grounds.

"They'll let you alone," he'd promised. And he'd seen to it that they had. The cattle had already been brought down by the time he and Keith arrived, so the cabin wasn't being used and old Mick Cardenal, who owned the place then, had been happy to let Luke and Keith use it.

It was too early for hunting season, but they rode and loafed and fished. Luke taught Keith how to tie flies. Neither of them shaved. Both of them drank a lot of beer.

"When I die," Keith had said sleepily one afternoon, lying under this very tree, "I hope heaven turns out to be southwestern Colorado."

"What makes you think you're going to heaven?" Luke had said.

Keith had opened one eye halfway. "Because I have always led a pure, unblemished, undefiled existence. Why else?"

Luke had tossed a rock at him. And they'd both burst out laughing. . . .

Now, two years later, Luke lay staring up through those same branches at another cloud-dotted Colorado sky.

"So, is it?" he asked Keith softly. "Is heaven like southwestern Colorado?"

"Who you talkin' to?" asked a childish voice behind him. Luke jerked up to see Paco standing there, holding the reins of Jimmy Kline's smallest horse. "You talkin' to God?"

Luke sat up straight, flushing. "What're you doing up here?" he demanded.

The boy shrugged narrow shoulders. "Running away from home."

"How come?"

"Too many girls." Paco wrinkled his nose. "Mama yells and Nelida bosses and Elena tags along all the time." Nelida was his older sister and Elena the younger. Luke didn't know them well, only enough to be glad he'd had brothers. "Can I live with you?"

"No."

"Why not? You got room. I could help you with the cattle. I'm a good rider. An' I can cook. Scrambled eggs. Toast. Bacon. I help Mama in the mornings in the café. Or I did," he added with a frown, "until Nelida bossed me out."

"Why'd she boss you out?" Luke asked, trying not to smile.

Paco took his question as an invitation to stay. He tied the horse and began balancing on a fallen log. "'Cause she's dumb. She says I broke the toaster, but I didn't. I fixed it."

"Does it work?"

"It would if she'd let me finish." Paco reached the end of the log and turned around and walked carefully back again. Hank followed him. Paco jumped off, picked up a rock and hurled it into the river. "I hate her. How come you were talkin' to God?"

Luke had hoped Paco'd forgotten that. Fat chance. He shrugged his back against the tree. "I was just muttering."

Paco threw another rock, then walked to the edge of the bluff overlooking the river so he could see where it hit.

"Get away from there," Luke said. "You could damned well fall in."

"You'd save me," Paco said.

Luke snorted. "I'd wave adios, *chico*. Get back now."

Paco made a face, but he went back to the log and started balancing again. "So how come?" he persisted.

Luke sighed. "'Cause I got a woman bossin' me around, too."

"Jill."

Luke blinked. "How do you know?"

"She told you to make tapes about Keith."

"How do you know?" Luke demanded again.

"She told me."

Had she told the whole damned world before she left?

"How many you done?"

"None. Zero. Zip. *Nada*."

Paco's eyes widened. "She's gonna be mad."

"I'll do 'em," Luke said gruffly. "It isn't exactly a piece of cake, talking into a machine."

"Talk to me."

Luke grunted. But it wasn't a totally stupid idea. In fact, it was a whole lot better than doing it by himself. He could answer Paco's questions. And Paco wasn't likely to ask anything he wouldn't be willing to answer. "Okay," he said.

"So, I can live with you." Paco beamed.

"I didn't say that!"

"But if we're gonna talk—"

"It doesn't take all day. Your mother needs you. You help her with breakfast."

"I'll help you. Please." Paco's dark eyes were beseeching.

Luke looked away. He picked up a rock and flung it savagely into the river. He ground his teeth.

"Remember in *The Thunder Rolls*," Paco said, citing one of Keith's best known movies, "where that kid, Jeremy, wants to stay with Keith on the boat—"

"It's not the same. It was a movie, for cripe's sake."

Paco cocked his head. "So it can't be true?"

"It can be," Luke admitted after a long moment. But he didn't want it to be. He threw another rock. And another. "Your mother won't let you," he said finally, hopefully, after a long moment.

"I'll ask her." Paco grinned.

* * *

She said yes.

"For three days," Paco told him the next afternoon. He looked disappointed as he reported the time limit that his mother had put on his stay with Luke. But then he brightened. "Maybe I can talk her into longer. I could break another toaster."

"Not in this life," Luke warned.

He was sitting on the steps of the cabin in the cool shadow of the evening, whittling a piece of soft pine. He tried not to show the dismay he felt. It had nothing to do with the kid personally, but Paco'd never believe that. Luke gouged his knife into the soft wood.

The boy scowled as he clumped up the steps carrying his sleeping bag. "You could at least say, 'We'll see,'" he grumbled.

"We'll see," Luke said dutifully.

Paco looked back at him over his shoulder. "You're just sayin' that."

Luke winked. "We'll see."

Paco grinned. "I'll get a tape and we can start."

It had sounded like a good idea yesterday. But now, faced with the prospect, he didn't want to do it any more than he ever had.

"C'mon. It'll be fun," Paco said. "I wanna know everything."

It wasn't fun. And Paco did damn near want to know everything. But having the kid ask him questions was easier than doing it on his own.

He reiterated for the tape the stuff he'd told Jill about how he and Keith had met. Then he told Paco about the first movie in which he'd actually doubled for Keith, about some of the stunts he'd done, which Keith had argued he ought to be doing himself. Luke talked his way through the movies they'd made in Portugal and India, in L.A. and New York, in Alaska and Tanzania. He talked about the good times. And talking about them to someone who was all eager ears and eyes was bittersweet.

It was so easy to remember how much fun it had been, how charmed Keith's life had seemed.

And, of course, how tragically it had ended.

He talked until long after the sun had set. He sat there on the porch as the temperature dipped, and Paco sat huddled and wrapped in a sleeping bag, asking questions. Overhead a three-quarter moon slowly rose to hang like a single silvery beam in a star-studded, navy-velvet sky. And still he talked.

He didn't see any of it. Not the child, not the sky, not the moon nor the stars.

He was seeing Keith—Keith laughing when the horse had bucked him off in Portugal, Keith waving his arms as the elephant's trunk curled around him and lifted him off the ground in India. He was remembering the way Keith had given him a thumb's-up sign after a rough-and-tumble bar fight in L.A., and the way he'd ridden a borrowed skateboard, standing on his hands, as they'd swooped through New York's Central Park. He was envisioning Keith, grinning like a fool through an ice-crusted mustache as he'd ridden behind a dogsled in Alaska, and a few months later, staring dreamily off into the sunrise on the Indian Ocean, his hand on the tiller of a traditional Arab dhow.

He remembered the utter stillness of the man and the moment.

And then Keith had looked over at Luke and smiled a crooked smile. "Who'd've thought a kid from Oxnard would ever come this far?" he'd said softly.

Or a boy from Bluff Springs, Colorado.

And who'd have thought that eight months later Keith would be dead, and that Luke would be back in Bluff Springs now?

He cleared his throat and jerked himself out of his reverie. "Do you know what a dhow is?" he asked Paco.

The boy didn't reply.

Luke looked around. Paco had been wrapped in his sleeping bag and was sitting behind him on the narrow porch, leaning against the wall of the house as he listened. He was still wrapped in the sleeping bag, still leaning against the wall, but he wasn't sitting any longer. He'd tipped sideways. His head was cradled in the crook of his arm, his lips were slightly parted, his eyes shut.

Luke studied him silently for a moment, then reached out and shut off the recorder. "That boring, was it?" he asked quietly.

Paco made a soft, whuffling sound. Luke set down his knife and the wood he'd been whittling. He got to his feet and brushed the wood shavings off his jeans. Bending down, he slipped his hands beneath the sleeping child and lifted him easily in his arms. Then he nudged open the door with his toe and carried Paco into the cabin.

He couldn't remember ever holding or carrying a child before. His own younger brother, Noah, was so close to his age that Luke had never carried him and, as an adult, he'd only been friends with guys like Keith, as childless as himself, and Carl, a widower whose children were grown.

It was a strange feeling.

The boy's warm, trusting weight felt oddly comforting as he crossed the room and settled Paco on one of the narrow bunks. He tucked the sleeping bag around him, then stepped back and stared down at the slumbering child, feeling an unwelcome, unaccustomed envy of those men to whom the weight of a child was commonplace.

He'd never felt such an envy before. Had never *wanted* to feel it.

Still didn't, he reminded himself sharply. He didn't want to be responsible for other people. He wasn't good at it. Fatherhood, like marriage, wasn't for the likes of him.

He did his penance. He made the tapes. It was easier—as he'd suspected—to do them with Paco's help. He liked talking to the boy, liked answering the boy's questions, telling him stories, making him smile.

But it was harder than he'd dreamed for exactly the same reason.

Because of Paco, Luke spent every day, all day in the presence of childish innocence and trusting naiveté that enchanted and pained him at the same time. With unfailing good cheer and eager curiosity, Paco, astride Jimmy Kline's gentle mare, followed him like a shadow everywhere he went. He held the wire while Luke stapled it. He chivied cattle out of the willows while Luke did the same. He even wanted Luke to teach him how to give an ornery old bull an antibiotic injection.

"You don't have to learn that," Luke said.

"I want to do what you do."

And so he did. And in doing so, Paco treated Luke to three days' worth of a view of the world unhampered by cynicism, by the constant plague of "what ifs" and "might have beens." There was none of that as far as Paco was concerned. He saw the world—the mountains, the trees, the cattle, the people—and it was good.

Luke didn't understand it. The kid had lost his father, for heaven's sake. He had a mother who was coping with three small children, struggling and just barely succeeding to make ends meet. His biggest hero was a man who'd died in his prime. He had to know that the world wasn't a carefree place!

But if he did, the knowledge didn't seem to dull Paco's enthusiasm.

He met every morning with a smile and Luke's cynicism with a shrug. And without seeming to try, he was worming his way under the cowboy's thick hide.

Pretty soon, Luke thought grimly the last afternoon of Paco's visit, the kid would have him whistling while they worked. He was already making Luke think about what it would be like to have children of his own.

It was a relief when Thursday night came and he could send Paco home.

"You sure there's nothin' you forgot to say?" Paco asked hopefully while Luke saddled the sorrel for him.

"I'm sure."

Paco came to stand beside him. "What about when you guys climbed that monument in New York? You didn't tell me much about that."

When he and Keith had scaled the Soldiers' and Sailors' Monument on Riverside Drive, Paco meant. Something Luke was relatively certain Paco's mother wouldn't want her law-abiding son hearing more about. "I told you enough," he said gruffly.

"How 'bout when you climbed those cliffs in Aca..." Paco's brow wrinkled as he tried to remember "...Acafulco?"

"Acapulco. And you heard enough about that, too." Luke tightened the cinch and tucked the sack of tapes in the saddlebag.

"What about the catacombs, then?"

"I thought you were asleep when I talked about that!"

Paco shook his head. "Are there really passages under New York City?" He was looking wide-eyed and eager, ready for a story.

Luke grunted. He'd said enough on the tape about the time he and Keith had sneaked down beneath the campus of CCNY and did a bit of underground exploring while they were there shooting a movie. He didn't suppose Paco would be going to New York any time soon, but he didn't think Linda would thank him for giving the kid ideas about that, either.

"Enough," he said. "Go get your sleeping bag and I'll tie it on."

Paco went, grumbling. "You're just tryin' to get rid of me," he said when he came back.

"Yep." Luke lashed the sleeping bag onto the back of the saddle, then nodded at Paco, waiting for him to get on.

Paco stalled. "Don'tcha get lonely up here?"

"No."

"Never?"

"Never," he lied. "Come on. Get on and get moving. You'll be down at Jimmy's before dark. He'll run you into town. Ask him to mail the tapes to Jill while he's there, okay?"

Paco looked doubtful.

"Just do it," Luke said, giving the boy an impatient look that finally had Paco scrambling up into the saddle.

"If you say so."

"I say so." Luke dug in the pocket of his vest. "Here." He handed Paco two small figures he'd carved. A man and a boy, each on horseback. Paco's eyes lit up as he examined them. Then he lifted his gaze to meet Luke's.

Luke shrugged. "It's you and Keith."

Paco looked at them more closely. He shook his head. "Nope. It's me and you."

He didn't wait to watch Paco head down the hill. As soon as the boy started, Luke turned on his heel and strode toward the cabin. He went in and shut the door.

He was alone.

He sank down onto his bunk and sucked in the silence. This was what he wanted—space, quiet, solitude. He didn't need Paco. He didn't need anyone. It was far better like this, to be accountable to no one, beholden to no one. Alone.

He lay down on his bunk and stared at the wooden ceiling over his head, then turned his head and looked at the stripped-down bunk where Paco had slept the past three nights. It looked unusually bare.

"Better this way," Luke said aloud.

The kid was gone. The debt was paid.

He breathed deeply and let the air out slowly. He was free.

He got up off the bed and started to make himself some dinner, trying to get back to normal, to think about tomorrow, about the cattle, about what needed to be done.

He wondered what Jill would think when she heard the tapes. He wondered especially what she would think of the last few minutes. He'd debated a long time about them. Finally he'd decided that he owed her.

He hadn't been able to forget the way she'd looked at him when they'd talked about why he'd kissed her. He'd tried to put it out of his mind. He couldn't. He could still see the pain and bewilderment in those wide gray eyes. He'd already caused her more than enough pain. That little bit, at least, he could erase.

He knew he wouldn't have had the guts to say it even then if Jill were anywhere around. But she was safely back in New York.

So last night, after Paco was asleep, Luke had taken the final tape back outside. He'd sat on the steps in the dark and turned the recorder on. It whirred almost imperceptibly in the silence for several moments before he began.

"That's pretty much it," he'd said finally. "That's Keith the way I remember him. The way I want to remember him, at least." He paused and stared out into the darkness. "There will never be another like him. I owe him the best years of my life."

Hank came and laid her head on his knee. He scratched her behind her ears, swallowed and went on, wishing his voice didn't sound quite so ragged. "I'm sorry that things turned out the way they did. Believe me, nobody can possibly be sorrier than I am." Another pause. Longer than the first. *Say it, damn it. You owe her.* "And I'm sorry I treated you the way I did, too." This time he jammed his finger on the pause button.

Damn, this was difficult. He took a deep breath. And another. Then he turned the recorder on again. "It wasn't because I didn't like you," he said. His fingers tightened in Hank's soft fur. "It was because I did."

He stopped and considered erasing that, then let it alone. He owed her that much honesty.

"That's why I kissed you, too. I just wanted you to know." He stopped then. There, that was enough. Wasn't it? No, it wasn't, and he knew it. He didn't just owe her for the kiss. He owed her for what he'd said to her the last time he'd seen her, too.

He cleared his throat, then paid his debt in full. "What I said to you the other day…it was a lie. I didn't want just any woman. I wanted you."

Four

He had the sun in the morning and the moon at night—and sixteen-hundred head of cattle, give or take a few, to look after every hour in between.

It was what he wanted, Luke reminded himself. Work, and lots of it. And no human beings depending on him.

He threw himself into it with renewed determination.

Any cowboy worthy of the name knew that the better part of moving cattle where you wanted them to go was letting them think the destination was their own idea. A buckaroo with brains just sat back and let them go, ambling along behind them, hedging up alongside only when they begin to drift. He damn sure didn't push them.

Luke did. He didn't seem to be able to leave well enough alone. He didn't seem to be able not to make work out of what should've been as natural as breathing.

It was because he didn't have Paco there, plaguing him with an incessant barrage of questions. It was because just loafing along gave him too damn much time to think.

He didn't want to think.

So he made work. He moved cattle. He checked gates. He rode fence. He cut quakies and dragged them back to the wrangle pasture so he could replace some of the rotted rails in his corral fence.

He liked to tell himself that it helped. It didn't. Not really. Not much.

He was grateful—and he was damned sure the cows were—when he actually did have some real work that kept him on his toes. He never thought he'd be glad to see one of his better bulls develop a stifle injury, but bringing the ill-tempered beast down to the corral where he could give him cortisone and then keep an eye on him was at least a challenge.

And once he got the bull in the corral, it took every bit of his concentration to get the animal more or less immobilized by roping him and tying him between two trees so he could dismount and try to get close enough to give him the shot.

The bull twisted and kicked, catching one of Luke's shins right above the boot with a well-aimed hoof.

"Sheee—!"

"Are you all right?"

The question came out of nowhere. Luke's head snapped around.

Jill was climbing over the aspen fence and coming toward him.

He hopped up and down, clutching his leg, furious at the sight of her. "What in the sam hill are you doin' here? You're supposed to be in New York!"

"No."

"You said you were going back to New York!" Outrage mixed with pain.

"I never said that, you just said I *could.*"

Which was true, he realized. Damn it all. "Get out of here!" he snapped. "What're you coming in here for?"

"He hurt you."

"He doesn't like people on foot."

"Then why were you?"

"Because I had to doctor him, and the damned horse has too much sense to get close enough." He rubbed his shin once more, then turned away and swung up into the saddle, ignoring her once he saw that she had climbed back over the fence.

He tried to pretend he was consumed with untying the bull. He could've gotten killed for all the attention he was paying.

God in heaven, what was she doing here?

Had she listened to the tapes?

Of course she'd listened to the tapes. She'd heard it all—including what he'd never have said unless he'd been certain she was two-thirds of the way across the country!

And now she'd come to... come to what?

With jerky, angry movements, he set the bull free, opened the gate and rode out of the pasture. "Shut the gate," he said tersely.

She did.

"I sent the tapes down. You got what you wanted," he said gruffly.

"Yes. Thank you." She walked over to the sorrel that she'd tied to a tree. She undid the reins and climbed into the saddle, then rode up next to Luke and sat there quietly, watching. Waiting.

She'd wait a hell of a long time before she heard him say anything as foolish as he'd said on that tape!

"Then you got what you came for. So why aren't you gone?"

"Because I like it here?" she ventured, giving him a smile that made his insides clench.

Deliberately he turned away from her and touched his heels to the sides of his buckskin, heading down the mountainside toward the cabin at a fast walk.

Jill followed.

He ignored her all the way down. He unsaddled his horse and turned him out, then limped toward the house, still without speaking. Jill kept right on coming.

When he got to the door he turned around. "Go home."

"No."

He ground his teeth. "What are you trying to do to me?"

"Talk to you. Get you to talk to me."

"I did my talking on the tape." And a damned fool he'd been to do it, too.

"You liked me." She said the words softly, wonderingly almost.

He scowled. "So?"

She smiled again. "I never guessed."

"You weren't supposed to."

"Why not?"

Was she dim, for heaven's sake? "Because, damn it, you were Keith's girl!"

"You . . . wanted me . . . all along?" She said that wonderingly, too, flushing after she said it, her eyes only connecting with his for a fleeting instant before looking way.

"Apparently," he said bitterly. "A man isn't answerable for his hormones."

"Is that all it was?"

"What do you want? A testimonial to your undying charms?" he snarled. "You want me to say I took one look and you knocked me on my ass? Fine. You did."

Her eyes widened then as if he'd shocked her. He hoped to God he had.

"Lust," he said succinctly. "I was horny, just like you said."

"But—"

"For you, okay? Not just any woman. I admit it. But it was wrong. And once it got the better of me, and I kissed you, and that was wrong, too!"

"Was it?"

Luke felt as if he could have heard a nickel drop in New York City. He swallowed, nonplussed, dazed, as if he'd just taken an unexpected uppercut to the jaw.

"Of course it was," he snapped when his wits returned. "We both know that."

She sighed. "Yes."

But she didn't say it firmly. His eyes narrowed and he looked at her closely. "What're you playin' at, Jillian?"

"Nothing. You're right. It was a mistake. And...thank you for telling me."

"Well, I didn't want you thinkin' I thought you were just a piece of..." He stopped, unable to even finish the sentence without offending her. And himself.

He jammed his fists into the pockets of his jeans and rocked back on the heels of his boots.

She nodded slightly. "Thank you," she said again.

"You're welcome." *Now, go,* he urged her silently. *Get on your horse and go!*

She didn't. She ran her tongue over her lips, chewed briefly on the bottom one as she stared down at her boots. Then she lifted her gaze again. "I have a confession to make, too."

He just looked at her. He couldn't imagine that it was anything he wanted to hear, but he knew she wouldn't damned well leave until she'd said it.

He didn't reply at all, just waited. Far overhead he could hear the faint roar of a jet on its way to Denver. Close by he could hear a magpie in one of the trees, scolding.

"I liked it."

His mind went blank.

"I liked your kiss," she said when he didn't respond. Her voice was low, but firm. Her eyes met his, frank and guileless.

His teeth came together with a snap. "Is that supposed to make me feel better?"

She took a step back. "Obviously, whether it was intended to or not, it doesn't."

"Smart lady."

"Am I?" she said almost bemusedly. "If I was, I don't think I'd be up here now."

"So why are you?"

"Because I admired your honesty. Because I felt I owed a similar honesty to you."

"Yeah, well, you've paid up, thanks very much, so you can go away now."

She didn't. She stayed right where she was and tilted her head as she looked at him. "So... was this honesty of yours a one-time deal, then?"

"What's that supposed to mean?"

"You're acting like you hate me. Again."

He shrugged irritably. "Force of habit?" he offered finally, reluctantly, embarrassed.

She laughed. "See if you can break it."

He shook his head quickly.

"Scared?" She gave him a mocking look.

He felt a muscle tick in his jaw. "What do you want, Jill?"

She hesitated, then shrugged and gave him a faint, almost-wistful smile. "I want you to kiss me."

He stared at her, certain he hadn't heard correctly. But she was just standing there, waiting, and then he was certain that he had.

"God Almighty, woman, how can you want that? I *killed* your fiancé!"

Jill said something rude and succinct and wholly out of character. He looked at her, shocked, and she stuck out her jaw as if defying him to make something of it. "I mean it, Lucas. And you know it, too. Keith died, but you're the one who's not living. You've shut yourself off completely up here like a hermit."

"I'm fine."

"You deserve more."

"I have what I want."

"How do you know?"

He yanked his hat off and rubbed a hand through his hair. "I know."

"Then why won't you kiss me? Are you afraid you might like it?"

"I know damned well I'd like it!"

"Well, then . . ."

"I can't!" Not and be certain that he could stop, that he could control the need that had been building in him practically since the moment he'd laid eyes on Jillian

Crane. Not and be sure he wouldn't betray Keith even further.

"You can't?" The look she gave him would have undermined the resolution of hundred stalwart men.

Luke steeled himself against it, against her. "No."

"Well, then—" she gave a tiny shrug and a shake of her head "—I guess I'll just have to kiss you."

"Don't! Jill, you can't—!" He took a step back, then another.

It was no use. She kissed him.

Luke was not unaccustomed to having women take the initiative. There was a certain breed of women who preyed on men who did dangerous stuff for a living, especially lean, good-looking ones with heavenly blue eyes and a devilish smile. He'd met his fair share during the years he'd spent cowboying, but they were a mere handful compared to the legions he met once he started doubling for Keith.

Being kissed was nothing new to Lucas Tanner. He'd always been able to handle it. He'd always been able to handle *them*. He never, *ever*, felt out of control.

There was always a first time.

This was it.

The moment Jill's lips touched his, the instant he felt her hands slid up the thin cotton sleeves of his shirt, felt her fingers grip the muscles of his upper arms, the second the fullness of her breasts brushed against the wall of his chest, he lost it. Totally.

Willpower? He acted like he'd never heard of it.

Common sense? An entirely foreign term.

He only had one thought: Jill.

She consumed him the way a fire consumes a forest. If their first kiss had kindled his desire, this one sent him down in flames. All the best intentions in the world seemed powerless against it. Against her.

Maybe it was because he'd been resisting so hard. Maybe it was because he had wanted her for so long. There was no way he could even think about it rationally. He could only feel.

And what he felt was good.

It felt good the way her lips touched, then tasted his. It felt good to respond, to let his tongue tangle with hers, to make her, in turn, respond to him.

It felt good. It was good; but it wasn't good enough.

Luke needed more than her mouth on his. He needed his hands beneath the soft cotton of her blouse, sliding up on the petal-soft warmth of her back. He needed his knee nudging between hers, so that his thigh pressed into the juncture of her legs. He needed to feel the soft pressure of her leg against the arousal that strained against the denim of his jeans.

He needed Jill.

He didn't know which of them moved first. He didn't know who took the lead up the steps into the cabin, who opened the door, who kicked it closed after them. He didn't know whose fumbling fingers worked loose the buttons most quickly or whose fevered hands were fastest at skinning off the jeans they wore.

He'd never in his life felt this sense of desperation, of urgency. He didn't even stop to shed his boots. His jeans tangled in them and tripped him when he tried to bear her back onto the bed.

Gravity came to his rescue, and they ended up there anyway, their arms locked around each other, their mouths still nipping, seeking, tasting. But even the nips and the tastes and the delicious friction of flesh on flesh weren't enough. The hunger was unquenchable.

Luke had seen Jill in a bathing suit countless times. He remembered well the gentle curve of her hips as she walked down the beach. He recalled the swell of her breasts as she lay flat on the lounge and tanned. He'd spent more hours than he wanted to think about fantasizing just how those curves and swells would look if the bathing suit wasn't there.

And now he knew. He saw. He touched. With trembling fingers he traced the shape of her breasts, he teased them to peaks of arousal and felt her writhe between his legs.

"Luke! Oh!" And then she touched him, too. She brushed her hands down across the soft dark whorls of hair on his chest, then let them follow the trail that arrowed down his abdomen to his groin. She touched him there.

He groaned. Her name was a plea on his lips. He moved aside the vee of her legs and touched the center of her. She shut her eyes and arched her back. Her breathing became quick and shallow, as quick and shallow as his. The need surged inside him, thrummed through his blood, rushing, clamoring. He couldn't wait any longer. He'd been waiting years.

"Jill! I need— I've got to—"

She nodded frantically and drew him down to her, brought him into her. "Yesss! Oh, Luke, yes."

Yes. That's what it was. *Yes.* An affirmation. A connection. A tie to another human being. Not just any human being. Jill.

Jill, whom he had watched from afar. Jill, whom he had kept at a distance. Jill, whose smiles and understanding and faith had always been just out of reach.

But now, right now, she was his.

She was warm and sweet and slick, and she welcomed him eagerly. She smiled at him. She stroked his face and touched his lips, fitted her body to his. And in her arms Luke found heaven. Or at least he did until his passion ebbed and sanity returned.

And then he felt like hell for what he'd done.

He'd taken Keith's woman.

The one thing he'd sworn he would never do. The one thing he had managed *not* to do even when he'd wanted to. The one last shred of self-respect that he'd clung to— even when all the rest had deserted him—abandoned him now.

He rolled away from her, anguished and ashamed, and shoved himself off the bed. He yanked up his shorts and jeans, his fingers fumbling in his haste. He couldn't look at her. Couldn't even look down at himself.

"Luke?" Her voice was soft, questioning, worried.

And like a wounded animal, he lashed out. "Satisfied?" he asked her. "Is that what you wanted? How do I compare?"

She looked at him, stricken.

He spun away, unable to face the anguish on her face. She didn't say anything for what seemed like an eternity. He turned away.

He heard the cot creak as she sat up. She made no move to cover herself as she got off the bed. He didn't look at her, anyway. He stared out the window, his jaw clenched tight, his hands fisted inside the pockets of his jeans, as she picked up her clothes and put them on.

"Compared to Keith, you mean?" she said when at last she was dressed. She walked to the door and opened it, then looked back over her shoulder at him. "Compared to Keith, you're an ass."

* * *

It wasn't anything he didn't call himself. In fact, he called himself that and other things several thousand times worse over the next three days.

His anger was almost savage. He took an axe and practically mowed down an entire stand of quaking aspens. When he finished, exhausted and drenched with sweat, he rationalized that he had enough to replace the wrangle-pasture fence. He knew damned well he had enough to fence a quarter of Colorado, but he pretended he didn't.

It was really just a way to work off the fury and the pain he felt. Fury at himself for what seemed the ultimate betrayal of Keith's friendship. Pain at having to turn his back on what had been the most beautiful experience of his life.

When he dared remember the way he'd felt in her arms, the way she'd felt in his, the way she'd given herself so completely, so selflessly to him, he ached all over again.

But even as he recalled the sweet fulfillment of that brief connection, he knew he had had no right to pursue her. He'd always known it.

And yet he'd taken her. Taken her sweetness and her love, and then lashed out at her, blamed her for giving him what he'd wanted.

Oh, yes. He was an ass.

"You're lookin' kinda peaked. Cows been keepin' you up late?" Jimmy grinned down at him from the back of his big buckskin gelding.

Luke straightened up from the posthole he'd been digging and wiped a hand across his stubbled jaw. "They keep me busy." And if they weren't the reason he hadn't been sleeping this past week, he damned well wasn't telling Jimmy so.

"Brought the salt up." Jimmy jerked his head at the packhorse trailing behind him on which he had loaded five fifty-pound bags of salt. "Thought I'd better get on it now. Don't want to be out of shoutin' distance much longer. Annette's already big as Riley's barn and she's swellin' some. She's gotta stay off her feet till her time comes. And when it does, I better be there."

"Leave the salt. I'll put it out when I'm finished here," Luke said as he bent to the hole again.

"Naw, it's okay. She won't need me today. She'll be fine. Besides, Jill's with her—"

"What?" Luke's head jerked around.

Jimmy nodded cheerfully. "It's workin' out swell. She likes the peace and quiet, says she can get a lot of writing done. I don't see how, myself. She's always cookin' and bakin' and running to help out when Annette needs something. She even keeps an eye on Jimmy, Jr."

Luke rubbed a hand across his mouth, then spat out the dirt he'd managed to get in it. "Good for her."

"Er, it...ain't a problem is it, her stayin'?" Jimmy asked, apparently struck suddenly by the notion that Luke, as his boss and the owner of the ranch, might have something to say about it.

"I'm just surprised." He'd thought she'd be on the first plane out, desperate to put as many miles between herself and Lucas Tanner as she could manage.

"She's a trooper. Works like a Trojan. Wouldn't have figured it, a fast-lane lady like her. But she doesn't seem that way at all. She's just like regular folks. But then, I reckon you already know that."

Luke grunted. He didn't need her virtues extolled.

"Reckon she'd make a good wife. Wonder somebody don't snap her up."

"Keith was going to," Luke reminded him harshly.

A frown flickered across Jimmy's lean face as he reflected on that. "Yeah, right." He scratched his head. "Don't suppose you could maybe double for him with Jill, too?"

Luke slammed the shovel into an aspen branch so hard that the wood snapped. "Go put out the damned salt!"

He got most of the row of postholes finished, moved the bull out of the pasture, driving him back up the mountain so he could earn his keep with the cows, and moved a dozen or so cattle out of the creek bottom. He lost a calf that had fallen into the swift current of the river and, wet and cursing his bad luck, finally got back to the cabin after five.

Jimmy's horse was standing in front of it, reins hanging down.

Luke was surprised he'd stayed around. With Annette so close to her due date, he'd figured Jimmy'd hightail it home as soon as he finished. He dismounted, unsaddled and turned his horse out, expecting Jimmy to come out of the cabin when he saw Luke was back. He didn't.

It wasn't that uncommon for Jimmy to leave his horse untied to graze, but it was wholly unlike him not to loosen the cinch and let the buckskin have a breather.

Luke caught up the reins and rubbed the horse's neck. "Hey, fella, where's Jim?"

The horse stood placidly under his touch. He rubbed a hand down its side. The big gelding looked as if he'd been standing awhile. The sweat was already dry on his neck.

"Jim? Hey, Jimmy?" Luke gave a shout, then strode up to the cabin and poked his head in. Jimmy wasn't there. Luke muttered under his breath.

He changed quickly into dry clothes, saddled a fresh horse for himself and one for Jimmy, turned the buck-skin out in the pasture and headed up the mountain.

It took him over an hour, and he was well beyond the third salt lick, when he finally heard a faint reply to one of his yells.

"Here!" came a voice rough with pain. "Up here."

Luke spurred his horse up the hill. He could see Jimmy lying beside an outcrop of rocks, his hat off, his red hair disheveled, his face white with pain. His right leg lay crookedly and he winced as he tried to lift himself onto his elbows when Luke rode up. The packhorse was at the far end of the alpine meadow, still half-loaded with salt.

"Rattler spooked m'horses," Jimmy said. "They both ran off. Packer didn't get too far. I broke m'leg, Luke," he said miserably. "Mighta done my wrist, too."

Luke swung down and crouched beside him, running his hands lightly down Jimmy's leg. He could feel the displacement. It sent shivers down his spine.

"I'll try to bring the truck up."

Jimmy shook his head. "Help me on the horse."

"You can't—"

"Lemme try. At least lemme try. Give me a hand up."

Luke straightened. Jimmy held out a hand. Luke shook his head. "Let me lift you from behind. Your back okay?"

"Think so." Jimmy gritted his teeth as Luke came around and slipped his hands beneath his arms, then slowly and carefully began to raise him.

"Oh, hell—" Jimmy's breath whistled out as he bit off an expletive. Sweat broke out on his face.

"You gonna faint?"

"No." The answer came through clenched teeth. "Get me over to the damn horse."

Luke remembered the white-hot pain when he'd broken his leg in Spain. He could see it searing Jimmy now. He admired Jimmy's courage, admired his grit and determination. "Here now. You're up. Okay?"

Jimmy looked as if he was going to faint. "'Kay," he said numbly.

Luke swung back into the saddle. "All set?"

Jimmy, pale as death, gave a jerky nod of his head.

It was past dark when they got down to where the rutted trail down the mountain reached the narrow dirt lane. "I'll ride on ahead," Luke said, "and bring back the truck. You just keep comin'. Okay?"

Jimmy hadn't said a word all the way down the mountain, but it was too dark for Luke to see a nod, so he managed a "yes." Then, with supreme effort, he added, "Don't upset Annette."

Luke didn't have to. He could tell she was a wreck the moment he saw her face in the window, peering out anxiously, when he rode in. At first she'd looked relieved to see a rider. Then she opened the door, saw Luke, and the color drained from her face.

"What happened? Where is he?"

"He's okay. He broke his leg, that's all. He's coming. I'm taking the truck." He dismounted.

Annette was halfway down the steps. "I'm coming, too."

Luke took in her barnlike figure and the fact that she couldn't walk, only waddle. "The hell you are."

"He's my—"

"No."

"What's wrong?" Jill appeared suddenly, silhouetted in the doorway. When she saw Luke, her expression grew grim. She turned away from him, asking Annette, "What's the matter? What happened to Jim?"

"Broke his leg. Luke's going to get him in the truck. I want to go with him."

"Luke can bring him down better alone. Come on." Jill hurried down the steps and took Annette's arm. "You call the doctor. That way he'll be expecting Jimmy at the hospital."

Luke sent a silent blessing her way, grateful for her calm common sense and for the fact that she was already leading Annette back into the house. He followed them in and snagged the truck keys off the hook by the door. "I'll be back as soon as I can."

"Hurry," Annette urged him.

He started to reach out a hand to get Jill's attention, then dropped it. "Thanks," he said.

She ignored him completely.

He met Jimmy halfway, got him down off the horse and stretched out in the bed of the truck. Then he tied the horse onto the back and drove slowly down the lane toward the ranch house. Jimmy was holding his own when they got there. He slid forward on the truck bed until he sat on the gate. Annette was waiting on the porch.

"Oh my God," she said when she saw him. He looked paler than ever in the cold glare of the light atop the post near the house. He took hold of Luke's arm and tried to stand. He went down like a tone of bricks.

"Jimmy!" Annette shrieked.

Jimmy, Jr., sucking his thumb in the refuge of Jill's arms, started to cry.

Luke cursed under his breath. "He only fainted."

"Jimmy!" Annette was frantic now.

"He'll be all right," Jill said soothingly as Luke dragged Jimmy's inert body onto the truck bed again. "It's better that he's fainted. He won't feel the pain."

"But—" Annette was trying to clamber onto the back of the truck with him, pushing her way past Luke.

"Damn it. Get out of here!" Luke snapped.

Jill gave him a disapproving look and tried to catch Annette by the arm. "Let Luke take him. You shouldn't even be up, let alone exerting like this. You don't want to have this baby right now, do you?"

"I won't. Let me go! He needs me!"

"Ma-ma!" Jimmy, Jr. wailed in Jill's arms as his mother tried to push Jill away.

Luke let go of Jimmy and grabbed her by her shoulders. "Stop it. He doesn't need you now. Your baby's the one who needs you."

Annette stared at him, white-faced and shaking.

He scooped her up bodily and lifted her out of the truck, then set her on her feet, holding her steady. "All the way down the mountain, he worried about you. You and the baby. That was what mattered to him. Not himself. Understand? So you're not doin' anything that will jeopardize that baby."

"That's right," Jill put in, surprising him. "Let Luke take him, Annette. You come and lie down. You'll be of more use to him later."

Annette looked from Jill to Luke to the still body of her husband in the back of the truck. Silent tears ran down her face.

Jill slipped an arm around her and pulled her away from Luke. He let her go. "Shh," Jill said. "It's all right."

"I'm so bad at this," Annette said, her voice wobbling. "I'm supposed to be brave. Jimmy says ranchers' wives are brave."

"Has Jimmy ever been a rancher's wife?" Jill asked archly, and Luke couldn't help swallowing a smile.

Annette blinked. "What?"

"Never mind," Jill said. She gave Annette a squeeze. "You're doing fine. All you have to be is Annette. That's enough. Come on, now." She drew her toward the house. "Luke will call when he has news." She gave him a look that said he'd better.

"Soon as I know," he promised.

Annette hesitated. "I want—"

"Damn it!" Luke exploded. "I'm his boss. He got hurt working for me. I'll see to this. What if you go into labor? Jimmy said you've been having problems. What if you lose that baby?"

She looked at him, shocked.

"It could happen," he said ruthlessly. "Do you want to go through the rest of your life thinking you killed your kid?"

"Luke!" Jill's voice was furious.

But he was beyond caring. He glared at Annette now, wracked with his own guilt over Keith, over Tanner and Clare's baby, damned if he was going to let anyone else make a foolish choice.

Annette shrank back from his anger, seeking comfort along with her son in Jill's arms. "You'll call?"

"I said I would." Luke promised again, then met Jill's reproachful gaze. "Keep her here." Then he turned on his heel and headed for the truck.

Five

___

There were plenty of advantages to living in rural America. One of them was that the doctor you were taking your hired man to might be your brother-in-law by marriage. The disadvantage was that he might also be the man your ex-sister-in-law had married after divorcing your own brother.

Still, regardless of family complications, Russ Moberly would do his best, Luke knew.

He just had to get back from Durango.

"What the hell's he in Durango for?" Luke demanded when the starched white brigade met him at the door, loaded Jimmy onto a gurney and trundled him into the emergency room, transferred him to the X-ray table and left Luke to sit. And sit.

"He went to a golf tournament and banquet," the nurse on duty told him apologetically. Her name was Lucy Campbell and she'd been a couple of years ahead of him in high school. She'd been almost as reckless as he'd been in those days. Now she wore a wedding ring, and he could see photos of a trio of little girls tacked to the bulletin board behind her desk.

"And he didn't leave anyone to cover?"

"Dr. Milliken is here. But there was an accident on the highway just this side of the pass. He's operating right now." Lucy grimaced. "Then he's got another one. After that, it's Jimmy's turn. Don't worry."

He worried anyway. Not about Jimmy, but about Annette. He could still see her white-faced panic. He debated the merit of calling. He didn't have anything to report, after all. But he thought she'd probably worry more if he didn't.

Jill answered the phone. "How is he?"

"Doc's not here. At least Russ isn't. The doc who's covering for him is workin' on somebody else."

"So I can't tell her anything?"

"You can tell her not to worry. Hell, it's just a broken leg."

"Another time she might find that comforting. Right now she's been depending on him, looking to him for strength, and he fainted right in front of her."

"Not on purpose!"

"I know that," Jill said, "but she's emotional. It's the pregnancy. She can't help it."

"Well, make her help it, damn it!"

"By bullying her into it the way you do?"

"I never claimed to be a nice guy."

"What, and lie?"

Luke's teeth snapped shut. He deserved it; he knew it, but it didn't make it any easier to take. Out of the corner of his eye he caught sight of movement down toward the operating room.

"Gotta go," he said. "I'll be in touch when something happens."

Nothing did for hours. It was well past two in the morning when, almost simultaneously, Doc Milliken finished with his second accident victim and was able to deal with Jimmy and Russ Moberly shouldered his way through the door and tossed his jacket on the counter.

"Golf banquet?" Luke said to him.

Russ flushed. "Once a year. And they're tearing up the pass. Let's have a look at you," he said, turning to Jimmy.

At last things began to happen. It was a nasty break. It would need surgery. On that both Doc Milliken and Russ agreed. The wrist was broken, too, but not as badly.

"We'll just cast it," Russ said.

"It's my ropin' hand," Jimmy muttered, then moaned as they settled him back onto the gurney to move him to the operating room. "Call Annette," he instructed Luke as the doors opened and then began to swing shut behind him. "Tell her I'm fine."

But when Luke rounded the corner into Admitting to use the telephone, he found Jill.

"I thought I told you not to bring Annette down! Take her home! Damn it, you get her down here, all riled up, and what do you think she's going to do?"

"Have the baby."

"Damn right. So—"

"Too late. She's having it."

He blanched. "The baby? She's havin' the baby? *Now?*"

"They've taken her down to be prepped."

"She can't!"

"I'm sure when you're God you'll do a better job of arranging the universe. In the meantime," Jill said acid-

y, "even without your permission, Annette is having the
baby."

"Jimmy's just gone into surgery," he argued, not that
t made a damn bit of difference.

"I'll tell her."

"But—"

But Jill had turned her back on him to talk to the admitting clerk, another woman he'd gone to high school
with. Jill finished giving the clerk—Nancy, he remembered her name was—the information that Annette must
have given her on the way into town. She didn't look at
Luke again. He might as well have vanished right off the
face of the earth as far as she was concerned.

It might not have been a bad idea from his point of
view, either.

He felt like a man standing in the eye of a storm. He
didn't connect with reality again until he noticed that Jill
had finished and was heading down a corridor.

"Hey!" he called after her.

Nancy, the clerk, glared at him. "For heaven's sake,
Luke! This is a hospital!"

"Sorry," he muttered. He strode down the hall after
Jill.

Nancy leapt out of her chair and went after him.
"That's maternity! Only fathers are allowed. You can't
go down there!"

He glanced back. "You gonna stop me?"

He caught up with Jill as she reached the labor room.
"I want to tell her myself. It was what I told her I'd do."

Jill looked at him, then nodded and stepped out of the
way. "By all means."

The minute he stepped into the room he had second
thoughts.

Annette was lying half propped up in a hospital bed, her hair as woolly and wild as a sheep at the end of a long, cold winter. Her face was colorless except for a high flush along her cheekbones, and her eyes were huge and smudged.

"Jimmy?" she asked, her fingers white as they clutched the bed rail.

"In surgery."

"Is he in a coma?"

"Of course not." Then he remembered that the last time she'd seen her husband, he'd been out cold. He rested his palms on the rail at the foot of her bed. "He came around before I even got him to the hospital. Really, Annette, he's— Are *you* all right?"

The last burst from him because as he was speaking she began to shift uncomfortably. Her hands went to her abdomen, her lips tightened into a thin line, her whole body grew tense.

Jill brushed past him and leaned over her. "Relax, Annie. Breathe slowly. Deeply. Easy now. Easy."

Luke, who in his time had delivered his fair share of calves, found that watching human labor wasn't nearly as sanguine an experience.

Annette tried to take a deep breath. It had a ragged edge and with it came a small moan.

"Steady," Jill said softly. "You're doing fine. Just fine."

Sweat beaded on Luke's upper lip. "Are you sure?"

Jill shot him a hard glare. "If you're going to say things like that, get out of here."

"I was only asking," he protested. "Maybe I should get a nurse."

"The nurse is just outside. She's got another mother to attend to. Here, give me a hand."

He blanched. "I deliver calves, not babies."

"Not that kind of help," Jill said impatiently. "We have a doctor for that. I mean help her breathe. Rub her back."

"You want me to...rub her back?"

"Purely platonically," Jill said, giving him a hard look. "Don't worry. You'll be quite safe."

Then Annette began to have another contraction and Jill turned abruptly away, giving Annette all her attention, urging the woman to match her breathing. The contraction passed. Annette rolled onto her side. Jill reached over the bed rail and rubbed her back.

Luke watched. He saw her hands move in slow, even, rhythmic strokes over Annette's back, and he remembered the way those same hands had touched him. His eyes traced the profile of her bent head, the fall of her hair as it curved behind her ear, saw the tip of her tongue jut out for just a moment and run across her upper lip. And he remembered the way her hair had brushed against his chest, the way her tongue had touched his lips, had tangled with his tongue.

His fingers clenched around the bed rail. He stifled a groan.

Jill slanted him a glance.

"Here it comes again," Annette said, and he saw her try not to tense as the contraction overtook her.

"Doing fine," Jill murmured, still rubbing. "Just fine."

"I'll do it," Luke said suddenly, needing to do something.

Jill looked doubtful, but he stepped forward, and she moved aside and let him take over. He rubbed Annette's back, and it was purely platonic. But he couldn't help what his mind was thinking. In his mind the skin he touched and stroked and kneaded was Jill's. Annette let out a sigh of something—relief, bliss, momentary freedom from pain? Luke didn't know. What his mind heard was the eager whimper that Jill had made when she was loving him, being loved by him. He flicked a glance in her direction.

She was watching his hands. Her breathing was shallow. Her lips were slightly parted and seemed to tremble.

"I gotta go," he said abruptly, and he jerked his hands away from Annette and took off out of the room without looking back.

"What happened? Is he...all right?" Annette asked.

There was a second's pause. Then he heard Jill answer, "I think he went to check on Jimmy."

He'd totally forgotten about Jimmy. But it seemed a good idea—and a way of salvaging his sanity. For the next hour he shuttled back and forth between maternity and surgery. There was no way he was going to start touching Annette again, not when all he could think about was touching Jill in entirely more intimate ways. Finally Jimmy was out of the operating room and in recovery. Annette seemed to relax more after that, and Jill favored him with a fleeting look of approval.

Around five in the morning, Jimmy recovered from the anesthetic and the tables turned. One of the nurses, thinking she was being helpful, told him that Annette was in labor, and at once Jimmy tried to get up to go help her.

"The hell you are," Luke exclaimed. "You're staying right here."

"But she needs me! She's counting on me. It's my kid!"

"She's got Jill. They're doing fine."

"You sure?" Jimmy sagged back against the bed. "Thank God for Jill," he murmured. He shut his eyes for a moment, then looked at Luke once more. "Go see how they're doing, will you?"

So for the next hour and a half, Luke went back and forth bearing reports the other way.

Annette moved into transition finally, needing to pant, becoming frantic and clinging to Jill's hand, squeezing it so fiercely Luke thought the bones would break.

But Jill never faltered. She brushed Annette's hair away from her face, blotted her cheeks and forehead with a cool damp cloth, all the while keeping up the soft words of encouragement that Annette needed to steady her breathing.

"Time to move to the delivery room," Annette's doctor decided at last.

He asked Jill to come along. "She'll do better if you're there," he said. Then he turned to Luke. "Guess you might as well come, too, if you're reporting back to Dad."

"Me?" Luke gulped. "But I—"

Annette's gaze fastened on him. "Please. For Jimmy."

He wanted nothing more than to back right out of the room and keep on going. He was nailed to the floor by Annette's beseeching blue eyes. He gave one small, jerky nod of his head. She beamed. Then the beam turned to a grimace, and she clutched Jill's hand.

"Oh, God! I need to... I need to push."

"Let's go," the doctor said.

Luke thought that cows had it better. No one told them they had to move right when they were in the throes of delivery. No one hustled them from bed to gurney to delivery table while they agonized. But then, no cow, to his knowledge, had ever had Jill to help her through it. And Jill was an asset, no doubt about it.

She steadied Annette by her mere presence. She spoke calmly and soothingly all the while the doctor and nurses did their bit. She kept Annette focused, stroked her cheek, brushed her hair out of her face, let her fingers be mashed by Annette's desperate ones.

Luke watched. And felt as useless and out of place as a steer in a pen full of heifers. He wasn't sure exactly when the faint, queasy feeling and the perception that things were getting stuffy turned into something a little more pressing. One minute he was standing there, watching as Annette strained to push with the contraction, and the next he felt a rushing sound in his ears and he took a desperate step back toward the wall.

"Oh, hell," he heard the doc mutter. "Get him outta here."

And the next thing he knew he was out in the corridor, sitting in a chair with Jill pushing his head down between his knees.

"Deep breath," she said. "Now another."

He dragged in the air, felt himself shudder, heard the rushing sound in his ears fade gradually. He stared down at the linoleum between the blue gauze sanitary shoes they'd made him put on over his mud-caked boots. In the distance he heard a baby crying.

"All right now?" Jill asked, and he managed a nod, embarrassed to death.

"I'll just go back in then. See if we've got a girl or a boy making all that racket."

She was long gone before Luke realized that the baby crying must be Annette's. He lifted his head slowly and slumped back against the chair, closing his eyes. God, what a jerk he was.

He could hear people talking and moving around inside the delivery room. Above them all, he could hear a baby. Furious and indignant. But alive. Thank God for that.

He took another deep breath, then two. He needed to go back in—if they would let him. He needed to get all the particulars and go tell Jimmy. But he could well imagine the reception he'd get. Luke Tanner damned near fainting at the sight of a baby being born? Hell, he'd never live it down.

Maybe if he waited, a nurse would come and tell him.

When the door opened finally, Luke straightened and looked up hopefully.

It was Jill. "Better now?" she asked.

He stood up quickly, his cheeks still burning. Immediately, he wished he hadn't; he was still dizzy and had to grab the doorjamb for support. Jill started to reach for him, then tucked her hand into the pocket of her slacks.

Luke swallowed and took a deep breath. "I'm fine. Just got a little light-headed, I guess. Must've been hungry or something."

She didn't call him a liar. She just nodded. Then she smiled. "It's a girl."

He'd forgotten about the baby. Now he grinned. "Sounds like a banshee."

Jill laughed. "She's a fighter. Annette will have her hands full, I'll bet." Her laughter faded and she smiled again, almost wistfully. "Lucky girl," Luke thought he heard her say. She looked away.

"I'll go tell Jimmy," he said.

"Come see the baby first. Then you'll be able to report firsthand." She opened the door to the delivery room and held it.

The nurses smiled. The doctor looked up from whatever messy business he was engaged in and grinned knowingly at him.

Luke shrugged sheepishly.

"Where'd you go?" Annette asked. She was pale but composed now as she lay on the delivery table looking up at him, her baby cradled in her arms.

Luke shrugged awkwardly, feeling heat creeping into his face. "I just . . . needed some air."

Annette's eyes widened. "You mean you had to . . . *you* . . . got sick?"

"I did not get sick!" he retorted, then grinned at the knowing looks. "Much."

Annette giggled. "Wait'll I tell Jimmy!"

"You do and you'll be living back in town," Luke threatened, but she just laughed again.

"You won't kick us out," she told him confidently.

"Yeah, well, not if you keep quiet about it," he said gruffly, then edged closer to get a look at the baby. "Not bad," he said. "Little more wrinkled and redder'n a calf, but—"

"Lucas Tanner! She's beautiful," Annette protested, hugging her sleeping daughter close.

"Whatever you say. Got a name yet?"

"Jimmy and I are going to have to talk about it," Annette said, then her eyes widened and she levered herself up slightly. "How *is* Jimmy?"

"Doing fine. And probably antsy as hell waiting for news."

"Go then," she urged him. "Tell him she's seven pounds eleven ounces, twenty inches long, has lots of beautiful brown hair, lovely blue eyes, and she's absolutely gorgeous."

"She is? Er, yes, ma'am." Luke gave her a grin and a wink and started for the door.

Jill was standing in front of it. She looked tired and disheveled and more beautiful than ever.

And, God help him, even now he wanted her.

Their eyes met, and he knew she didn't want him—or anything to do with him.

Taking a deep breath, Luke brushed past.

The sun was already well above the mountaintops by the time he'd talked to Jimmy, relayed all the messages about his new daughter and reassured him that Annette was doing fine. He was just heading out to be the first customer in Paco's mother's café when he looked up to see Jill coming out of Annette's room.

"Everything okay?"

She nodded. "She's sleeping. So's the baby."

"So's Jimmy."

"Good," she said. She looked as if she might go past him.

"You okay?" he asked her.

"I'm fine." She gave him a wan smile. He shifted awkwardly from one foot to the other, wondering what else to say. Jill leaned back against the wall and shut her eyes briefly.

"You must be beat."

She opened her eyes and rubbed the back of her neck. "First delivery I've ever been through. Takes a lot out of you even when you aren't the one doing the work."

"You were pretty impressive. You got her through it."

"She needed me to."

"You're calm in a crisis."

"Not always," she said, and he knew they were both remembering Keith's death. It was always there between them.

He set his hat on his head and tugged it down. "I gotta go. There's a ton of work to be done."

She hesitated, then said, "I'm going to get breakfast at Linda's. Do you want to come?"

He wanted to; he didn't dare. And thank heaven this time his stomach didn't growl and betray him. "Naw," he said, even as he realized what it must have cost her to invite him. His mouth twisted. "Thanks anyway. Maybe some other time."

Jill didn't answer. She started toward the door.

"Jill."

She turned halfway around.

"About what I said the other day... I'm sorry."

Jimmy would have been irrigating in the morning in the south field. He would have been mowing hay in the north later that afternoon. He would have fit in fixing the gate by the Peelers' place somewhere in between. Luke didn't get down the mountain to work on the irrigation until past three.

First he had to feed the dogs and horses, haul the salt, check the cattle, move a bunch up out of the willows, doctor a calf that had pinkeye, shut a gate some hikers had left open and ride an extra two miles just to check another gate he was sure he'd have to open if they left it shut. They had. He did. So by the time he finally rode into the yard by the ranch house, it was already midafternoon.

Jill's rental car was parked by the kitchen, so she was back from the hospital. He didn't go into the house. He turned out his horse, then took the truck and headed for the fields.

Cy Nichols, his neighbor down the highway, was already there.

"Ran into Jill in the café this morning," he said, lifting his hat and running a hand through thin, gray hair. "She told me what happened. We figured we'd help out." He jerked his head toward the far side of the field, and for the first time Luke spotted a small form hunkered down alongside one of the ditches. Paco.

"He's a worker, that one," Cy said, blue eyes crinkling in his sun-weathered face. "He'll make a good hand."

"I expect he will. Much obliged to both of you."

Luke did the irrigating. Paco fetched and carried. Cy started the mowing. "That's enough for today," Luke said when Cy finished the first field. Then, stomach growling and back aching, he remembered the gate.

"Need a hand?" Cy asked.

Luke shook his head. "Thanks for all you've done."

Cy dismissed his afternoon's work with a wave of his hand. "We'll be back tomorrow." He ruffled Paco's hair. "Come on, boy, time we got you home for supper."

"Told ya I could help," Paco said to Luke out the open pickup window.

Luke gave him a tired grin. "I reckon you did."

He watched Cy's pickup disappear down the road in a cloud of dust. Then he straightened up, got in his own truck and headed for the gate.

It was past seven when he loaded his tools and drove back to the house.

He saw with surprise that Jill's car was still parked by the kitchen. He figured she'd have gone into town to see Annette and Jimmy and the baby.

He probably ought to drive in himself, but he was dirty and sweaty and hungry, and he hadn't slept in thirty-odd hours. He didn't think he had the strength to ride back up the mountain, clean up in the creek, ride back down and drive into town.

He could shower in the house. But doing that meant seeing Jill. He didn't do it.

He picked up his saddle and bridle, and was heading toward the corral when he heard a shout behind him.

"Hey, Luke!"

He turned to see Russ and Clare's eleven-year-old son, Dan, leaping off the porch and coming toward him.

"What're you doing out here?" he asked when the boy got close.

"Staying."

"Staying? Here? How come?"

"'Cause Mom went to California for a school-nurse conference and Dad had to go to Denver for some state meeting, so Aunt Annette said me an' Kevin could stay with her."

"Annette's in the hospital."

"Yup, I know. She had a girl. We saw it this morning when Mom took us and Jimmy, Jr. in."

"So Annette can't take care of you."

"I know. Jill is. She said it didn't matter, since she's got Jimmy, Jr. anyhow."

Luke tried to digest that. He'd thought Clare and Russ would be keeping Jimmy, Jr. not the other way around. "She's got all three of you?"

Another nod. "We're helping. I coulda helped you today with the irrigating, but you left so fast, we didn't even know you were here until you were halfway up the road. Can I help you tomorrow?"

Luke felt light-headed again. He dragged a hand across his face. "Sure. I guess."

"I'll be ready. Want some dinner?"

Luke blinked. "What?" he asked, but his stomach had heard this time, even if his mind was still sorting out the rest of what Dan had told him. It wasn't letting him turn down a meal again. It growled loudly.

Dan grinned. "We're finished, but there's lotsa leftovers. Jill said you could have some."

Did she? And what had prompted that?

"I don't think so," he said, and his stomach registered an immediate protest. He pressed a hand against it.

"You want me to tell her you're not hungry?"

Luke sighed. "Maybe I could go for a little something." But he took his time following Dan to the house, and all the way there he was certain he was making a mistake.

He was right.

It didn't matter that he knew she had every reason to hate him. It didn't matter that he hated himself. It didn't matter that she wasn't a bit glamorous or even conventionally pretty as she stood at the sink washing the dishes, with Jimmy, Jr. clinging to her jean-clad knees and Russ and Clare's younger boy, Kevin, revving Matchbox cars back and forth across the floor behind her.

He still couldn't take his eyes off her.

She, on the other hand, was apparently cured of any lingering interest in him. She barely flicked a glance his way, then shut off the water and picked up a towel to wipe her hands.

"You want something to eat? I'll reheat the stew," she said briskly. "And make some biscuits."

Luke bent the brim of his hat in his hands. "Don't go to any bother."

"No bother," Jill said flatly. She scooped the baby up with one arm and set him down to play with Kevin. Then she opened the refrigerator, ignoring him.

He deserved it. He knew that. It didn't help much.

"Er, reckon I oughta clean up a bit. You mind if I take a shower?"

Her gaze raked his dirty- and sweat-stained jeans and shirt, his grubby, unshaven jaw and disheveled hair. "It's your house. Anyway, I'd say the time would be well spent."

Luke flushed. He nodded his head jerkily and headed upstairs to the bathroom. Once there, he stripped quickly and submerged himself beneath a stream of hot running water. It was bliss. So much bliss that he almost fell asleep just standing there. Only when someone turned on the hot water downstairs and he got a sudden spurt of cold did he jerk himself awake and stumble out to dry off.

There was no sense putting his dirty clothes back on, since he kept most of his clothes down here anyway. Tucking a towel around his waist, he made his way down the hall and into his bedroom.

He stopped dead and stared. One of Jill's blouses was hung over the back of the rocking chair in front of the window. A pair of sandals poked out from beneath the bed. A suitcase was tucked beside the dresser. A hairbrush, some lipstick and a pair of earrings lay on top of it. Jill was living in his room.

Jill spent each night sleeping in his bed.

He ran his tongue over suddenly dry lips. His fingers clenched against folds of the towel around his waist. He looked at the bed and tried to imagine her there, her head on his pillow, her body curled beneath the quilt—the quilt that was the only thing he had left from his mother.

Deliberately, he turned away from the bed—from the thought. He fished a shirt off a hanger and pulled it on. He grabbed a pair of shorts and some jeans out of a drawer and pulled them on. He sat down on the edge of the bed to pull on his socks. When the mattress gave under his weight, he felt himself sag, too.

The day and the night and the day caught up with him. The trek down the hill with Jimmy, the night in the hospital, the surgery, the baby's birth, the cattle, the irrigation, the gate.

Jill.

He sighed. His fists tightened against the worn denim covering his thighs. He dropped his head back and stared at the ceiling. It wasn't the ceiling he saw. It was Jill.

He could hear her now, saying something to Kevin and Dan, then laughing at their reply. They laughed, too. He heard Jimmy, Jr.'s high-pitched giggle and remembered the way Jill had looked with Kevin playing underfoot and Jimmy, Jr. hanging onto her legs. Comfortable. In her element. Maternal. Gentle. At ease and capable with the children just as she had been with Annette last night. More examples of what a good mother she'd have been. If only...if only...

Once more it all came back to that.

There was no end to the memories, the might-have-beens. There never would be. He sank back on the bed and gave in—just for a moment—to the bone-wearying fatigue that overcame him.

Six

It was already light when he opened his eyes. For a long moment he didn't remember where he was. Then he did. And groaned.

He was lying on his bed—*Jill's* bed. He'd sat down to pull on his socks before going down to eat supper how many hours ago? He didn't even want to think.

It didn't matter. Supper was a dead issue. God, how could he have done that? And where had Jill slept since he'd taken her bed?

A glance around showed him that she hadn't shared it with him. There was only one dent from one body. He finished yanking on the socks he'd started with hours ago, then fumbled with the buttons of his shirt on the way to the bathroom. Then, combing his hair with his fingers, he hurried down the stairs.

"Good morning."

She was already up, sitting beside the high chair, feeding Jimmy, Jr. some cereal. She was wearing the same jeans and shirt she'd been wearing the day before. He wondered if she'd gotten any sleep at all.

"Sorry," he muttered. "I didn't mean to crash like that."

"You'd been up a day and a night and a day."

"So had you."

"I caught forty winks yesterday when Jimmy, Jr. took a nap."

"That's a lot," Luke said sarcastically.

"I'm fine. Besides, it wouldn't have done me much good to go to bed. Jimmy's been fretful. He's teething."

"So you've been sitting up with him all night?"

"I was down on the couch at first. He woke up about four and I went up and gave him a bottle. We fell asleep in the rocker." She flushed slightly.

"In my—in *your*—room?" She'd sat there and watched him sleeping? "You should've kicked me out!"

"You were sleeping like the dead. Besides," she added, "it's really your room."

He figured she had realized that, but her saying it made him feel awkward just the same. "You've been using it. You should've woke me up. Or... you could've lain on the bed, too. It's big enough."

"Sleep with you? Hardly."

He scrubbed a hand down his face. "Aw, hell, Jill. I said I was sorry about that. I never meant... You gotta know I didn't mean... what I said." He looked at her beseechingly. She looked back at him, her expression noncommittal. "I was angry at myself," he said. "Not you."

She looked as if she might argue, then simply shrugged. "You're going to have to come to terms with it eventually, Luke."

"I have."

She just shook her head, then turned away from him and opened the refrigerator.

"There's hot cereal on the stove," she said. "I can make you eggs and bacon."

"Cereal's fine." He dished up a large bowlful, added milk and ate it while he stood at the sink. He put two pieces of bread in the toaster between spoonfuls and was glad when they popped up just as the cereal was done. He buttered them, then washed them down with a cup of coffee.

Jill finished feeding Jimmy, Jr. and got up.

Luke rinsed his dishes, set them on the counter and grabbed his hat from the chair where he'd left it the night before. "See you around," he said and opened the door. He got halfway down the steps and turned back. "I told Dan he could work with me this afternoon. I'm going up the mountain now. I'll be back down at dinnertime."

"It'll be ready."

"No," he said quickly. "I didn't mean that."

He fed the dogs and horses, then circled up the mountainside to check the cattle. Some needed moving, two needed doctoring. He brought a steer down to the pasture where he'd had the bull before. It had a long cut on its flank that he wanted to watch for infection. Doing only what needed to be done took him all morning.

He could have taken all day, but he knew that Dan would be waiting, and so would all of Jimmy's work. Still, it was nearly one-thirty by the time he got back down.

Jill came to the door as he stepped onto the porch. "Cy and Paco came by and got Dan. He said he'd wait for you to start the haying, but they'd be opening ditches in the west field."

"God bless him." Luke started toward the truck.

"Here." When he turned, she thrust a good-size sack and a thermos in his direction. "I've made your lunch. You have to eat," she said almost gruffly.

He took them. "Thanks."

He ate in the truck on the way to the field. She'd packed him three roast-beef sandwiches, an apple, some carrot sticks and half a dozen chocolate-chip cookies still warm from the oven. Inside his lunch sack was another plastic bag filled with more cookies. On it she'd stuck a note: "To share with the rest of your crew."

Luke smiled, knowing how welcome they'd be.

He was right about that. Cy and Dan and Paco were more than willing to take a brief break while Luke took over the tractor. Then they all went back to work, the boys on the ditches, Cy and Luke on the mowing and raking, until suppertime, when Cy said he'd better get going because Mary would have his hide if he was late and her soufflé fell.

"Mary makes soufflés now?" Luke remembered Cy's good-natured wife as a top-notch meat-and-potatoes cook.

"Oh, sure. Gotta branch out now we're retired." Cy winked as he walked to his truck. "Keeps us young."

"You reckon wearing yourself out helping me keeps you young, too?" Luke asked.

"Of course." Cy climbed in and started the engine. "I'll see you tomorrow. Let's go, Paco!" he called to the boy, who was skipping rocks in the creek with Dan.

"Aw..." The reluctance in Paco's face was obvious.

"Let him stay for supper. I can bring him in later. Gotta run in and see Jimmy and Annette, anyhow."

Cy nodded. "He'd like that. I'll tell Linda."

"Thanks. And thanks for the help. Don't know how I'd manage without you."

Cy shrugged. "It's what friends are for." He gave a wave of his hand, and the truck rumbled off.

Jill had supper simmering on the back of the stove when they got to the house, and it was served up on the table by the time they were washed and dried and ready to dig in and eat.

Luke didn't argue. He knew all about protesting too much.

He sat at the head of the table where she pointed. She sat at the foot, with Dan and Paco on one side and Kevin and Jimmy, Jr. in his high chair, on the other.

They talked and laughed, and Kevin spilled his milk. Paco said he didn't like green beans and Jill told him to eat three bites. Luke backed her up without even thinking about it until he'd done it.

Like she was the mother and he was the father. Like they were a family.

The sharp pain of realization bit him suddenly and without warning.

He didn't *want* a family. Even a pretend one. Even a temporary one.

He shoved his chair back and stood up.

"I got some things that need doin' in the barn. Send Paco out when you're finished and I'll run him into town when I stop at the hospital." He carried his dishes to the sink, dumped them in the dishpan, then pushed open the door. "Oh, and . . . thanks for supper."

He figured he'd give Paco half an hour or so, then head for the truck. The kid wouldn't keep him waiting much longer than that, and it would mean he wouldn't have to go back into the house looking for him.

He didn't. Paco was waiting. So were Jill and Dan and Kevin and Jimmy, Jr. The bigger boys were all sitting in the back. Jill had fastened Jimmy into a car seat in the cab. She was sitting next to the door.

"We're coming, too," she said.

Luke opened his mouth to argue with her, took one look at all the boys' expectant faces and got in the truck. At least there was a toddler between them.

The baby had a name.

"Julie Elizabeth," Annette announced when they arrived en masse to see the sleeping, considerably less red and wrinkled baby.

"A big improvement," Luke said to the infant as he bent over her small bassinette and looked down at her. "You might get a date to the prom, after all."

"Luke!" Annette tossed a magazine at him.

"Hey," he grinned, fending it off. "It was a compliment."

She made a face at him. "Go bother Jimmy," she said. "Let us girls have a chat."

So Luke took the boys, minus Jimmy, Jr. who was sitting on Jill's lap, into the other wing of the hospital, where Jimmy was propped up in his hospital bed. The boys were suitably impressed with his cast, especially when he invited them to autograph it. But within minutes they grew bored.

"There's nothin' to do in here," Paco complained.

"You're telling me," Jimmy grumbled. "I want to go home."

"Go play catch on the lawn," Luke suggested. When they were gone, he asked, "When will they let you out?" It couldn't be soon enough as far as he was concerned.

"Day after tomorrow," Jimmy replied glumly. "They had to split the cast because of the swelling. Probably won't get to put another on until tomorrow night or Saturday morning. Then, man, I'm outta here." Jimmy stretched his hands over his head, then dropped them gingerly into his lap. His shoulders slumped. "But even then I'm not going to be good for much."

"We'll keep you busy," Luke promised.

"I can't ride. I can't rope. Hell, I can't even write my name. And I didn't get to help Annette with the delivery."

"They did all right without you."

"They did fine," Jimmy grumbled. "Women can always do it without us."

Luke grinned. "Not all of it."

A reluctant smile creased Jimmy's tanned face. "Well, yeah, there is that." Then the grin faded. "But I didn't mean that. I meant, bein' there. I wanted to be. It's—I dunno—part of bein' a dad."

"I wouldn't know." Luke paced over to the window, caught sight of the boys out on the lawn and abruptly turned away from them, too.

"You ain't gettin' any younger, Luke," Jimmy reminded him with more intuition than Luke would have given him credit for.

He didn't answer. He stuffed his hands into the pockets of his jeans and shifted from one boot to the other.

"Nice name, Julie," he said at last in an effort to distract Jimmy. "Named her after Julie Sutter, did you?" He grinned. Julie had been one of Jimmy's early steadies. She was married herself now and lived in Texas. "I'm surprised Annette let you."

"Wasn't after Julie. We wanted to name her after Jill, but we didn't want to confuse things, so we picked Julie instead. It's pretty close."

Luke stared at him. "After Jill? Confuse what?"

"Oh, we figured it might be awkward havin' two of 'em around. Not even a Junior, like our Jimmy is, you know?"

Luke didn't know. "What the hell are you talking about? Jill's not gonna be around. She's just here to work on her book."

"Yeah, but—"

"Then she's leaving! Going back to L.A. or New York or wherever! Good grief." He muttered this last under his breath, trying to mollify his outburst somewhat as he paced around the small room. He stopped at the foot of the bed and fixed Jimmy with a hard, narrow gaze. "How come you thought she was staying?"

Jimmy just looked at him and shrugged.

He wondered if Jill knew they'd sort of named the baby after her. He didn't ask, but he slanted her several glances once they were all packed into the truck for the trip back to the ranch.

She was poking her head out the window, telling the boys to sit down and keep their hands in. They were waving to friends at the local spring-fed swimming pool as they passed on their way to drop Paco off at his house.

"Let's go swimming!" Dan yelled.

"Hey, let's!" Paco shouted, and Kevin added his cheers.

Luke ignored them.

"Please!" Dan called. "How 'bout it, huh?"

"Please?" yelled Kevin and Paco.

Jimmy, Jr. yelled, too, and clapped his hands.

Luke drove on past, went all the way up the lane where Paco's house was and pulled up in front.

"Can we go tomorrow night?" Dan asked when Luke shut off the engine and they all climbed out.

"We've got haying to do."

"We can work late," Dan said. "It's Friday. The pool's open late. Please? We're comin' in anyway to see Annette and the baby. Besides, it'll feel good on our muscles. My dad says that soakin' in mineral water is good for your muscles." He gave Luke an ingenuous grin.

"Prescribes it, does he?" Luke grumbled.

Dan nodded eagerly. So did Kevin. And Paco.

Luke looked at Jill. She didn't say a word.

"We'll see," he said at last.

"Yea!" Kevin yelled. Then he looked at Luke, his expression slightly sheepishly, as he explained, "That's what Mama says right before she says yes."

Luke's muscles were definitely in need of a long, hot, mineral-water soak by seven-thirty the following evening. He'd wrestled enough cattle and horses and tractors and bales of hay that day to give him a personal interest in the well-being of each and every muscle he had. Still he was reluctant to stay at the house for supper, then afterward take the kids and Jill to the pool.

So why was he doing it?

Because he felt responsible, he told himself. Dan and Kevin might have been left with Jill, but they were left on his ranch, in his house. And he felt responsible for Jimmy, Jr. because Jimmy worked for him. And he felt responsible for Jill because . . . because . . .

For a man who didn't want any responsibilities, he sure had a hell of a lot of them right now. But they were temporary, he assured himself. On Monday Clare and Russ would be back. Annette and Jimmy would be home even sooner. Tomorrow morning. And Jill would leave. Soon.

One night wasn't going to kill him.

It might even be fun.

It might be too much fun. It might be too easy to enjoy it, to find himself wanting those responsibilities for himself, to find himself wanting to be part of a family.

He was afraid of all that when they parked in the swimming pool's parking lot, and Jill took Jimmy, Jr. with her into the women's dressing rooms to change while he took Dan and Kevin into the men's room with him.

Dan leapt into the pool at once, barely missing two other boys who were playing water tag. Kevin stood on the side, then looked over his shoulder at Luke.

"It's okay," Luke said. "Go on."

"You come, too," Kevin said as his brother surfaced and splashed water at him.

"Later," Luke promised. He sat down on one of the lounges and dropped the towels in a heap.

"Come on, chicken," Dan called his brother. "Jump!"

Kevin sat down and dangled his feet in the pool.

Jill appeared just then, her tall slim figure as tempting as he remembered it, even though this time she was carrying Jimmy, Jr.

Luke remembered the last time he'd seen her in a bathing suit. The weekend at Big Bear. His jaw tightened.

"See?" she was saying to Jimmy, Jr. "There's Dan. Let's go in with him."

"'Nnn!" Jimmy, Jr. shrieked, slapping his hands against Jill's shoulders. "'Nnn!"

She put him down on the edge of the pool next to Kevin, then sat beside him briefly. "Ooh, it's warm," she said, flipping a quick smile over her shoulder at Luke. Then she slid off the side into the water and turned to take Jimmy, Jr. in her arms.

"Can I stand there?" Kevin asked her nervously.

"Not quite," Jill said. "Let's move down here." She edged away toward shallower water. Kevin went with her and slid carefully into the pool. Dan dove and plunged around them like a playful dolphin. Luke watched.

"Hey, Luke! C'mon in!" Dan urged.

"Yeah, c'mon!" Kevin called. He was jumping up and down, too, now, confidence growing.

"Naw." Luke shrugged. "I'm tired." He looked away, but in doing so caught Jill's eye. She was watching him, her expression concerned. His jaw locked and he deliberately looked the other way, then turned over and stretched out on the lounger, ignoring all of them.

"Lookit me, Jill! Lookit, Luke!" he heard Kevin shriek a few minutes later.

"No, look at me!" Dan yelled. "Jill, look! Luke! Watch!"

Luke heard Jill cheer, then laugh. "What a splash!"

He supposed both boys must have been doing cannonballs by that time.

"Watch me now!" Kevin called. "Watch this!"

"Terrific!" Luke heard Jill say after another huge splash.

"Now me!" There was another shout, then another. And pretty soon it sounded as if half the kids in Bluff Springs were clamoring to have Jill watch them.

Luke rolled over finally, feeling guilty for turning all the responsibility over to her. He looked where she had been, then discovered that she had moved and was now standing in the pool almost at his feet. She still held Jimmy, Jr. in her arms, while she watched Dan and Kevin and half a dozen other kids as they took turns jumping. As she watched, she shifted the baby from one arm to the other, then after a few minutes, shifted him back again.

"I'll take him."

Her head jerked around. She looked up at him. "What? Oh—" she smiled at him "—thanks."

He hunkered down beside the pool and reached for the boy as Jill lifted him up. But the moment Jimmy felt himself being taken out of the pool, his face screwed up and he started to cry.

Jill laughed. "I guess he doesn't want to get out just yet." And she took him back and cradled him against her side. "I'll keep him awhile longer."

"He's too heavy for you."

Jill shrugged. Their gazes met. He saw gentleness in her gaze. He saw understanding—understanding of feelings that, until this very moment, he hadn't even known he had.

He hadn't been in the water—except in his dreams—since Keith had died.

He sat down on the edge of the pool now and dangled his legs. The water was warm and soothing, just as Dan had promised. Still he felt reluctant. It was so easy to remember.

But Jill remembered, too. Slowly he pushed himself off the side and slid down into the pool until he stood next to her.

She smiled. *Don't,* he wanted to say.

He held out his arms. "Give him to me," he said, and he took Jimmy from her.

"Practicing, Luke?" He looked up to see Lucy Campbell from the hospital.

"Just helping out," he said.

"Fatherhood becomes you." She gave Jill a conspiratorial smile. Jill flashed Luke a half guilty, half worried look—a definitely apprehensive look. But before anything more could be said, Paco appeared.

"C'mon in!" Dan yelled.

Instead of running and doing just that, Paco squatted down on the edge of the pool and looked at Luke with dark, serious eyes. "I can't swim. Will you teach me?"

"Me?"

"You swam with Keith. You told me about bodysurfing. You said he was a champion."

"He was. I'm not."

"But you swam with him."

"Not in competitions."

Paco looked wistful. "I'd ask my dad, but I don't got a dad."

Oh, hell.

"Here," he said to Jill. "Hold Jimmy."

Luke wasn't much of a teacher, but Paco was determined. The trouble was, he was also obviously scared stiff. His lean young body went rigid in Luke's grasp. His fingers dug into Luke's arms. His breath came fast and shallow.

"Relax. You gotta relax," Luke said. "Here. I'll hold you. I got my hand under your belly. Feel it? Now stretch out and stroke forward. I'm not gonna let go. I promise."

"You s-sure?" Paco stuttered, trying to stroke, his movements jerky.

"I'm sure. Here, forget that. You gotta get used to the water a little. Come on, hang onto my back and I'll swim with you."

"Not where it's deep!"

"Not where it's deep," Luke promised. He took Paco onto his back and felt the boy's arms come around his neck like a death grip. "Loosen up a bit," he gasped. "You'll choke me."

"S-sorry." Paco loosened his grip fractionally. Luke began a slow, easy breaststroke, with Paco riding along.

"Can I ride? Can I?" Kevin yelled.

"Not now," Luke said. "You can already swim. Paco's just learning."

"I'll give Kev a ride," Dan said.

"And not drown him?"

Dan grinned. "Aw, shucks, how'd you guess?"

"I have brothers, too."

They shared a conspiratorial grin, then Dan promised, "I won't drown him. This time."

So he took Kevin on his back while Luke swam with Paco, and gradually, as they moved back and forth across the pool, the boy relaxed. He saw how much fun Dan and Kevin were having and he started to smile, too. He even bounced up and down like Kevin did and waved at Jill.

Luke looked over as Jill waved back. Then she grasped Jimmy, Jr. by his arms and twirled him around in the water, smiling at the little boy's giggles, then lifted him high into the air and snuggled him against her. Over the top of his head, her eyes met Luke's.

And her gaze held so much of what he wanted and feared that he couldn't look for long.

But if he couldn't look at her, other men could—and did. Mike Sutter's nephew, Garrett, and one of Sutter's hands, Dave Cole, had come for an evening swim and a chance to check out the available girls. It didn't take them long to find Jill.

The next time Luke paddled back across the pool with Paco, Garrett was standing next to Jill, holding Jimmy for her. He had the beginnings of a wolfish grin on his face.

"'Sa matter?" Paco asked when Luke tensed beneath him.

"Nothing." Luke stroked closer. "Splash Jimmy," he said to Paco.

"Huh?" Paco looked at Jimmy, Jr. and then at Garrett holding the little boy and all the time easing closer to Jill.

"Oh!" Paco, no dummy, splashed. He made sure he wasn't hitting Jimmy nearly as much as he was hitting Garrett.

"Hey!" Garrett yelped, turning to see where the water was coming from.

"Sorry," Luke said and gave them a bland smile. Paco grinned fiendishly.

But it wasn't as easy to do a second time, when Dave Cole moved in as well.

"You want to watch it," Luke said to Jill with deliberate casualness later that night as he headed toward the door.

The boys had wanted him to stay the night in the house, but he had dogs and horses to feed. And it was the better part of common sense not to hang around Jill too much.

She was sitting cross-legged on the sofa, drying her hair with a towel, and she looked up at him. "What's that supposed to mean?"

He shifted from one foot to the other. "Garrett and Dave. You want to, uh, be careful not to...not to...encourage them."

Jill looked at him from beneath the curtain of her hair. Then she shook her head. "They're nice guys."

Luke grunted, trying not to look at her. He didn't need to. He could close his eyes and see her smiling up at Garrett, see her laughing at Dave's stupid jokes. His teeth came together with an audible snap.

Jill's eyes widened. "Why shouldn't I encourage them, Luke?"

"Keith—"

"Keith," she said firmly, "would want me to be happy. You, of all people, should know that."

He knew it. But damn it... "With Garrett Sutter?" He fairly spat the name. "Or Dave Cole?"

"So give me another suggestion."

He couldn't. He had no right.

Seven

He was certain that once he got Annette and Jimmy and the baby home from the hospital, things would get better. Which went to show how little he knew. He couldn't disappear up the mountain and pretend that they could cope without the steer, because it was obvious they couldn't.

Jimmy didn't have a walking cast, but at least he had a cast that wasn't split anymore. Still, he couldn't drive the tractor. Nor could he do the baling. He couldn't even hobble along and open the dams of the irrigation ditches.

"I can help. I'll ride," Jimmy said. But if his leg dangled down too long, the swelling became far too painful, and the effort it took for him to get up on a horse's back in the first place made it unreasonable.

At least everyone thought so but Jimmy. "I'm not an invalid!" he bellowed fifty times a day.

"Stuff a sock in it," Annette told him. "Here. Hold the baby while I hang out the wash."

So Jimmy held the baby, balancing her gingerly against the cast on his broken wrist, looking like he'd rather run in the other direction. But at least it liberated Jill to help Luke in the fields.

"I don't need your help," he told her the first day she showed up as he drove out on the tractor.

"That wasn't you calling around noon looking for a hand to help out with the baling?"

He scowled, lifted his hat and rubbed a hand through sweat-drenched hair. "Know a lot about baling, do you?"

"I grew up on a farm in Iowa."

He stared. "I didn't know that." He'd always thought her innate elegance came from a sophisticated background.

"You can take the girl out of the hayfield, but you can't make her totally forget it. Although I have to admit, I have four brothers who helped a lot more than I did. And it was in Iowa, so it might not be the same. But I think I could manage to be of some use if someone was willing to teach me." The look she gave him was a direct challenge.

"What about your book? Don't you have a book to write?"

"I'm almost finished. Want to read it?"

"No." He started the tractor engine again. "Come on. Get on."

"Ah." Cy grinned when they got there. "Now this sorta help is more like it."

Luke let her rake. She caught on to the tractor driving quickly. "It must be like riding a bike," she called as she drove past.

"Just don't grind the gears," he yelled back.

"No fear," she said, and promptly did.

Luke winced. He stripped off his shirt and wiped his face with it, then hung it on a fence post. "Come on, Cy. Let's get loading."

He reckoned if he worked her hard enough that would be the last he saw of her.

So the next day—and the next, and the next—he found her lots of work to do. Raking. Baling. Driving the bale mover. And every day she came back for more. And when she finished what he gave her, instead of retreating, exhausted, which she certainly had a right to do, she brought them food from the house, then went down and helped Paco with the ditches.

She worked long and hard and she helped a lot. Luke appreciated it, in spite of himself. He even managed to say so after she'd been working with him for more than a week.

It was almost suppertime that evening and they'd finished the haying at last.

He gave her a ride back to the house on the tractor, and when she got down, he said, "Thanks. You've been a good hand."

"Good farmer," she corrected with a smile, swiping her hair away from her face. She had taken to wearing a cowboy hat now, but it didn't quite tame the long strands. "I don't do horses."

"You ride."

"Like a sack of potatoes."

"I could teach y—" He stopped, aghast at what he had almost offered. "You do fine," he said gruffly. "Anyhow, you won't need to do horses in New York." And he started the tractor abruptly, heading it toward the shed.

* * *

Usually by the time he got in the house, Jill had grabbed a quick shower and was in the kitchen helping Annette get supper on the table.

But tonight she was nowhere to be seen. He didn't intend to notice. He certainly didn't comment. Not, at least, until Annette said, "Let's eat," and he discovered that it was only she and Jimmy and himself at the table, Jimmy, Jr. having already eaten and Julie sound asleep.

"Where's Jill?" he asked before he could stop himself.

"Got a hot date." Jimmy winked.

"She's going out to supper with Garrett," Annette announced with what seemed considerable relish.

Luke didn't say anything, just shrugged and sat down at the table and started dishing up.

It wasn't his business what she did. All the same, he couldn't stop himself from giving her a hard look when she came downstairs a few moments later, her long hair piled into an intricate knot on the top of her head, a few tendrils escaping to tickle her neck. Her lissome curves were no longer outlined in denim and chambray, but in coral-colored silk the likes of which Bluff Springs had never seen.

"*Wooo-weee!*" Jimmy whistled.

"Oh, envy," Annette murmured, shooting Luke a significant look.

He gritted his teeth, bent his head and sawed at his steak.

"Where'd you get that?" Annette asked.

"In New York."

Luke chomped down on a piece of steak. It figured. All that business about being an Iowa farm girl was obviously long forgotten.

"Reckon I better ask Garrett what his intentions are," Jimmy joked.

Luke ignored him. He wouldn't have looked up even when Garrett came to the door to get her, except Jimmy invited him in, then kidded him about going out with the second-most-beautiful woman in Colorado.

"I won't argue, only because Annette's a good friend," Garrett said, smiling at Jill in a way that said all too clearly who he really thought merited being number one. Luke's knife hit his plate with an extraordinarily loud smack.

Garrett glanced his way and his smile faded slightly. "I'm not poaching, am I? If you and Jill are—"

"We aren't," Luke said, and he shoved his chair backward so hard it tipped over. He ignored it on his way out.

Three days passed. Luke didn't go down to the ranch. No one came up. Cy had said he'd look in and take care of what he could, and since the haying was done, Luke felt justified in staying away.

At least he did until the evening of the third day, when he was sitting on the steps of his cabin, sipping an after-supper cup of coffee and whittling a coyote out of pine. He was appreciating the solitude and the serenity of his existence and determinedly not thinking about Jillian Crane and the effect she had on him. A glance down the mountain showed him a rider heading his way.

For a single instant, his heart leapt as he remembered Jill coming up before. But another long moment's scrutiny proved it wasn't Jill. It was a man. With two good legs. A man who sat a horse easily. Garrett?

Luke stood up, his fists curling lightly at his sides as he watched and waited. And then he saw who it was, his whole body relaxed and a grin spread across his face.

"Noah!" He came down the steps waving a hand at the rider, who waved right back and spurred his horse to move a little faster.

"Son of a gun, what're you doin' up here?" Luke demanded as his younger brother got within speaking distance. Rodeo bronc rider Noah Tanner didn't often make social calls as he moved relentlessly back and forth across western America in pursuit of the NFR gold.

"Just passin' through," Noah said now, swinging down out of the saddle. "On my way to Washington, then thought I'd stop and see Tanner and his brood." He grinned. "Mag's p.g. again. Did you know?"

Luke shook his head.

"They're both happy as pigs in you-know-what. Anyhow, I was within twenty miles and, hell, I figured I hadn't seen you in a long time, so why not? Besides Tanner said—" He broke off suddenly.

"Tanner said what?"

"Nothin'."

"What'd Tanner say?" Luke thrust his face right into his brother's and was glad of his extra two inches.

"Said I should see if you were okay," Noah muttered. "He was worried."

"Of course I'm okay. Why shouldn't I be? Since when did you two start playing mother hen?"

"Reckon Tanner has a time or two," Noah reminded him.

"Yeah. But you?"

Noah rubbed the back of his neck. "You weren't doin' so good the last time I saw you."

Right after Luke had bought the ranch and moved back to Colorado, he meant. Right after he'd spent months on the road, trying to forget the past.

"You looked like you'd got stomped by Mr. T," Noah went on. He meant the bull, Luke knew, not the television actor.

"That was then. I'm fine now."

"If you say so," Noah agreed equably. He didn't look completely convinced, but he let it drop. "Got any coffee goin'?"

"I'll make some."

"Appreciate it," Noah said. He turned his horse out while Luke went back to the cabin. Then, carrying his saddle, Noah came in and sniffed appreciatively. "One good thing about you havin' been a Hollywood hotshot, you learned how to make interesting coffee."

"This is good, old-fashioned Colorado coffee."

Noah made a face. "Left that behind, too, did you?" He settled onto one of the narrow beds and grinned up at his brother. "Didn't leave Jill, though, I see."

"I didn't bring her here!"

If Noah was surprised at his vehemence, he didn't let it show. "That's what she said. Said she had to track you to the ends of the earth before she found you."

"She what?" Luke stared at him.

"Said she'd been all over God's green earth lookin' for you. Paris. London. Hawaii. Said she was always just a little too late. So she just wrote the book without you, then gave it one last shot." He cocked his head. "You didn't know?"

"Uh-uh." What would he have done if she'd found him while he was still running? What would he have done if he'd opened his hotel room door in Paris or London or

Hawaii or any of the other places he'd tried to hide from himself and found Jill standing there?

Nothing more than he'd done already, he reminded himself savagely. He jerked up the coffeepot and began to pour.

"She's a looker, that Jill," Noah mused now, folding his hands across his trophy belt buckle and stretching out on the bed.

Luke got another mug down out of the cupboard. "How you doin' in the standings?"

"Tenth. Not as good as I'd like. Prob'ly not as bad as I deserve. I've had some lucky breaks, drew some good horses. Reckon I might make it to Vegas if things keep goin' my way. How come you're up here if she's down there?"

Luke expelled an irritated breath. "Why shouldn't I be? She's writing a book. I'm riding the range. I live up here. She's just staying down there."

"I don't think so," Noah said.

"What's that supposed to mean?"

"Means you're actin' just a little too snuffy, I'd say. Kinda like Tanner was before he reckoned he and Maggie could get hitched into the same harness and pull in the same direction without the world cavin' in."

"I'm not like Tanner," Luke said shortly. "He had a happy ending."

"You can, too, if you want one," Noah said. He sat up and leaned toward his brother. "It isn't impossible."

"You're turnin' into a hell of an optimist."

"Maybe. But it's true," Noah maintained. "Tanner'll tell you. You gotta go after what you want in life. You want Jill, go after her."

"I don't want Jill!"

"No?"

Luke turned his back and stared out the window. "Leave me alone."

"Ain't like you to be a quitter, Luke," Noah said quietly.

"You can't quit what you never started."

"Didn't you . . . start something?" Noah's words fell like stones into the silence. Luke wondered exactly how much he knew, how much Jill had told him.

Damn, had she spilled her guts to his brother? Luke went to stand in the doorway, his spine stiff, his knuckles tight on the door frame.

"You can't quit," Noah said to his back. "Cowboys don't."

He came, he flung his words of Western wisdom and, like he always did, Noah left.

His words, however, pricked at Luke at odd times during the next few days. He fought them off, ignored them.

There were such things as false starts, he told himself. He and Jill had had one of those. You weren't really quitting if you turned your back on those. You were just showing good sense. It was better this way—for both of them.

Besides, in time he would forget her. With Jimmy home and Annette getting her energy back, with Cy checking in every day and Clare calling to help out, Jill had probably already packed her bags and left for New York.

Maybe she'd left when he had, he thought.

Or maybe she was staying around—thinking about a relationship with Garrett Sutter.

"Damn it!" He had ridden right into an overhanging branch.

He shoved it away and rode around the tree, then turned his head as he caught sight of some movement just down the mountain through the trees.

At first he thought it was a wandering cow, though he hadn't seen one on the way up. Now he saw that it was a horse. One of Jimmy's horses. What the hell . . . ?

Touching his heels lightly to his own horse, Luke headed down the slope after it. Surely, with a broken leg, Jimmy hadn't been stupid enough to come looking for him and get himself bucked off. Had he?

Luke caught the horse's reins and started down the mountain, looking.

He heard her before he saw her. *Jill*. Which didn't bring the relief that it should have. She was in the pasture where she'd found him when he'd been doctoring the bull, the one where he had the steer now, the one he'd told her to stay out of on foot.

Obviously she was on foot now.

But it wouldn't matter with the steer the way it would have with the bull, and she didn't sound as if she'd been hurt, though she must have been tossed off.

By the time he reached the fence, he could see her clearly. She looked none the worse for wear as she backed toward him, edging over near the pile of quaky branches that he'd cut for the corral. She kept her eyes on the steer, which was still standing on the far side of the pasture in high grass, regarding her curiously.

"Stay there," she told him. "Just stay right where you are. Don't come any closer."

Luke sat silently on the horse and watched, his amusement growing as he did so. All too often around Jill, he had felt foolish, even when she hadn't meant to inspire any such feeling. It was comforting, since she clearly wasn't hurt, to have the tables turned for once.

He dismounted quietly, glad she was making so much noise she hadn't heard him. Then he eased his way over the fence, aiming to come up behind her.

"I mean it," Jill was saying to the steer, which had taken a step or two in her direction. "Don't come over here."

The steer, unused to being talked to in anything except four-letter installments dished out by irritated cowboys, looked at her as quizzically as a steer can manage to look.

Luke moved closer, still not speaking up, wondering what Jill would do if the steer decided to pursue his interest. He imagined her turning and running straight into his arms. He couldn't help it; he grinned.

She'd reached the pile of quaky branches now, and she picked up one of the short ones, waving it like an oversize baseball bat. "See this?" she said to the steer. "Want it right between the eyes? No, of course you don't. So just don't—"

But the steer did. He tossed his head and started toward her, first at a walk, then at a slightly faster gait.

"Don't!" Jill warned.

Luke, almost behind her left shoulder now, expected her to turn and run. She stood her ground and assumed a batting stance, for all the world as if she were Henry Aaron looking for his sixty-first.

The steer kept coming.

"Watch it!" Jill cried, stepping into her swing.

"For God's sa—"

She caught Luke on the follow-through—right between the eyes.

Not that he realized it at the time.

At the time all he saw was the swing . . . and stars.

The first thing he heard was Jill, half-hysterical, crying, "Luke! My God! Are you all right? Luke!"

He couldn't see her at all. The pain was blinding, but even if it hadn't been, his eyes were swollen shut.

"Oh God, I'm sorry! I'm sorry! Come on! We've got to get out of here. The bull's—"

"'S a steer," Luke mumbled.

"What?"

"'S not a bull," he managed to say, struggling to sit up with the aid of her arm behind his back. "'S a—"

"Steer? Why didn't you say so?" Abruptly she pulled her arm out and let him drop back onto the ground.

He groaned.

Immediately she was contrite. "I'm sorry. I still shouldn't have hit you. But if I'd known—" Accusation began to creep back into her voice.

"You made your point," Luke said gruffly. He tried to open one eye. He could barely manage to let a little light in. It hurt like hell.

"Can you stand up?"

He did, finally. His head felt as if it were going to come off. He couldn't keep his balance without her holding him up. So much for having the advantage. He groaned again.

"Let's get you to the horses." She helped him slowly over to the fence. The steer, curious again, was practically breathing down their necks by the time they got there. Luke dreaded having to bend down and climb between the wires, with reason. He almost passed out by the time he got to the other side.

"Can you ride?" Jill asked.

"I can ride," he muttered.

She insisted on holding onto the reins of his horse in case it decided to go somewhere other than the cabin.

Luke assured her that it wouldn't, but she was stubborn and he was in no shape to fight with her about it.

A tentative exploration with his fingers indicated that he had a lump the size of a goose egg between his eyes, and his nose was probably broken.

"Thanks," he said when they reached the cabin.

"You need to see a doctor," she said.

Luke couldn't imagine telling any doc in town what had happened to him. If his almost passing out in the delivery room was memorable, this ought to go down in Bluff Springs history as first-class folklore.

"No," he said. "I'm stayin' right here."

"But—"

"No," he said, and slid off the horse before she could argue further.

"Damn it, Luke. You need help."

"I need to be left alone." He could make out the cabin and moved toward it. "Turn out my horse and you'll have done your good deed for the day. Then go away."

"But—"

"Go on. You've got things to do, I'm sure." He turned back, not that he could really see her, but he could pretend. "Why'd you come up here, anyway? Something wrong down at the ranch?"

"No. I came to tell you I was . . . leaving."

Still, the news shook him. He took a stumbling step backward, then steadied himself, trying to ignore the sudden hollowness inside.

She hesitated, but when he didn't say anything, she went on. "Annette and Jimmy are doing all right and I got the book finished. So, well, I figured it was time. I . . . have an assignment I've been thinking about taking." She sounded casual.

"Good for you." He stuffed his hands in his pockets. He was glad he couldn't see her now. He wished she couldn't see him. Hell of a way to remember him, looking like he had a piñata for a head.

"I...talked to Carl the other night," she said after a moment. "He has a job he thinks you might be interested in." There was an oddly breathless quality to her voice.

"No."

"It's a western. Right up your alley. Starts filming in the fall and—"

"I said *no.*"

"Luke; you need—"

"I don't need anything, except to be left alone. No. Thank you." His fingers curled into fists. There was a hammer slamming against an anvil behind his eyes. He turned back toward the cabin, moving carefully, determined not to make a bigger fool of himself by tripping and falling on his face. "Goodbye."

Hank fussing at the door woke him. The other dogs whined, too. Luke felt like whining himself. It had taken him hours to go to sleep. He hadn't had any ice to put on his face, but he'd got water from the creek and used soaking compresses in an effort to get the swelling down. If it had worked, by the time he went to sleep the effect had been marginal.

His only consolation was that Jill was really gone. Finally he could begin to try to forget her. As he'd drifted off to sleep, the pain finally giving way to sweet oblivion, he'd allowed himself a sigh of something like relief.

But relief was short-lived. The dogs were going nuts.

"What the hell's the matter with you?" he snarled, hauling himself to a sitting position and fumbling to light the kerosene lantern.

Outside he heard a horse neigh and he cursed vehemently, certain that Jill had left the rungs of the fence down and the horses were off to the four corners of the earth.

Damn! He struggled to his feet as the dogs barking grew even more frenzied.

The door opened as he got the lantern lit.

Jill said, "I'm ba-a-a-ack."

Eight

"What the hell—?"

"You didn't imagine I'd leave you here alone, did you?" Jill asked. She came right up to him and studied his eyes in the golden light. He could barely make her out, even now. He gritted his teeth.

"I'd hoped," he muttered.

"Well, I wouldn't. You might have concussion. You really should see a doctor."

"Don't start," he warned, "or I swear to God I'll throw you out right now."

"You and whose army?" And she took his arm and dragged him back toward the bed. "Lie down. I've brought some ice." She looked around. "I'll put it in a plastic bag and wrap it in a dish towel." She glanced about. "Good. You have dish towels."

"How uncivilized do you think I am?"

"Don't ask."

He heard her moving efficiently across the room, heard the clinking of the ice. Then she came over and sat on the bed. He edged away. Gingerly she laid the ice pack across his eyes and the bridge of his nose. He sucked in his breath.

"Hurts?"

Like hell. "I've had worse."

"I suppose you have." He could hear the smile in her voice. "Shh, now. Just try to sleep."

He couldn't possibly sleep. Not with her right next to him. What did she think, that pain deadened desire? She needed to think again. Still, when she didn't move about, just sat quietly beside him while the ice did its numbing best, he found himself relaxing without trying to.

"You said you were leaving," he murmured, fighting to stay conscious.

"I changed things around."

"What things?" Conversation would help, he decided. It would keep him from feeling quite so cozy.

"I arranged to keep the rental car, canceled my plane reservations and told Annette not to give someone else my bed." He could tell that she was smiling again.

He breathed more easily, not at the smile but at the idea that at least she planned to leave, to go back down to the ranch.

"Not that I expect I'll be using it, really," she went on, just as if she'd heard what he was thinking. "I'm staying with you."

"No. I told you no."

"Wanna fight about it?"

He groaned.

"I'm truly sorry about this, Luke."

"For smashing my handsome face?"

"Yes." And he could tell from her tone of voice that she actually meant it. He reached up a hand and pushed hers away, moving the ice pack off his eyes as he squinted up at her. It was a mistake.

She looked like an angel, her disheveled dark hair like a nimbus around her face, and all of her lit in the soft golden light of the lantern. It made him want her all over again.

A ragged sigh slipped from between his lips. Gently Jill replaced the ice pack. He felt something soft brush across his hair once, then again. Her fingers? Probably.

Her lips?

God, he had to stop thinking things like that!

"Go to sleep," she told him. "Don't worry. I'll take care of the horses and the dogs in the morning."

He should have protested. He should have told her he could manage, but God, it felt so good, despite the pain, just to give in this once.

Once wouldn't hurt, would it?

He could regain the ground he was losing tonight when he felt better tomorrow.

Couldn't he? *Couldn't he?*

When tomorrow came she wouldn't let him out of bed.

If he hadn't used a lot of choice, four-letter words when it came to preserving his modesty, she probably wouldn't have even given in to him on that.

She hovered all day—except when she was out feeding the horses or checking the cattle. He was glad when she left to do it. But once she had, he worried all the time she was gone.

What did she know about moving cattle? She might be a farm girl by birth, but, hell, this was the woman who couldn't tell a steer from a bull! She'd kill herself out there.

He tried not to fret about it. He didn't want her to think he was that worried. But when three hours passed and she hadn't reappeared, he couldn't pretend indifference any longer. He hauled himself out of bed and reached for his jeans.

The door opened. "What on earth are you doing?"

"I was, uh—" He couldn't even come up with a convincing lie. He sank back onto the bed, weak with relief. "Worried," he muttered. "About the cattle. Did everything go all right?"

She nodded. "Of course, I didn't really do anything spectacular. All the fence was intact, so I didn't even get to pretend I could mend it. I know I was supposed to get the cattle out of the creek bottom, and I tried. But they didn't want to listen, and they were bigger than I was, so I wasn't a huge success as far as that goes. But I did get the horses fed." She shrugged, grinning. "I might be a farmer, but I'll never make a cowboy."

"Doesn't matter, does it?" Luke said. He laid back on the bed, his head still pounding.

"Might." Jill's voice was soft.

He shot her a wary look. "Don't," he warned.

"Don't what?"

"Push."

"Is that what I'm doing?"

"Aren't you?"

She flushed and looked away.

"Uh-uh. So forget it. Forget me."

"I can't."

"I'm not worth it, damn it. Besides, once you had me, you wouldn't want me."

"How do you know?"

He never should've started this. He'd hoped that by spelling things out, confronting her, he'd get her to turn tail and run. He should've known she'd be like a grizzly when cornered, ready to do battle. Hell.

"Because," he said, his fingers curling into the bedroll, "I'm not Keith."

"No," she said. "You're not."

"I'm not cheerful and eager and a regular damned Boy Scout."

A hint of a smile touched her lips. "That's for sure."

The muscles in his jaw tightened. "I don't make the kind of money he did or have the fans he had or anything else."

"True."

"So what're you doin' here?" Even he could hear the anguish in his voice.

She smiled once more and lifted her shoulders in a gentle shrug. "Beats the heck out of me. I must be a glutton for punishment."

The next morning he awoke to find her lying on the other bed. It was still very early. He didn't need a watch to tell him that. He could see better this morning.

He wouldn't need Jill to do his work for him. He could send her home.

He rolled over onto his side and propped his head on his hand and looked at her. She was asleep.

He'd spent so much of the time he was with her either trying to ignore her or fighting with her, that he'd had damn few chances to simply savor the beauty and gentleness that was Jill. It wasn't in the best interests of his mental health to do so now. He knew it. But he didn't seem to be able to stop himself.

And hell, at least he'd have the memory. When he was a crochety old codger still wrangling horses and punching cows, he could drag it out and look at it in his mind's eye again and again.

It was worth the risk.

She was lying on her back, one arm under her head, the other clutching the blanket against her chest. He really couldn't see all that much of her, except her face. It was enough. His eyes traced the soft fullness of her cheeks, then leisurely moved down the stubborn line of her jaw. His gaze lingered first on the dark brown half-moons of her lashes, then dropped to her mouth. He remembered kissing that mouth. He could remember its taste. And the memory brought with it a need, surging up unbidden and unwanted inside him. Stifling a groan, he fought it off.

But whatever sound he didn't manage to stifle woke Jill. She stretched and rolled onto her side, opened her eyes and looked at him.

"Good morning." The softness of her voice sent a shiver down his spine.

"'Mornin'." His own voice sounded rusty. He rolled up to a sitting position, knowing full well the danger of lying there looking at Jill lying there looking at him.

She sat up just as quickly. "I'll do it. You should stay in bed."

He slanted her a grin. "I appreciate the offer, but this is one thing you can't do for me."

Jill blushed as he tugged on his jeans and ambled toward the door. "You're all right?" she called after him.

"Fine." He was, in fact, much better. Not that he looked it. His face looked worse than the time a bull had caught him with a flying hoof back in his rodeo days. Not surprising. That had been a glancing blow. This had been anything but. His one consolation was that having to look at him ought to turn off any lingering interest Jill might have.

But if it did, she didn't show it.

By the time he got back, she was up and dressed and had the coffee on. He could smell it the moment he opened the door. It set his stomach to growling and he pressed a hand against his belly. All of a sudden he was starving. He said so.

"I don't wonder," Jill said. "You didn't eat anything yesterday."

He couldn't remember much about yesterday. Only that she'd been here fussing over him, that she'd gone to check on the cattle, that he'd worried until she came back, that he'd tried to make her see sense and that she hadn't. Obviously, or she wouldn't still have been here.

"Sit down. I'll make you breakfast."

It was too early to argue with her. He sat down and let her make it. She'd come equipped, that was for sure. He usually got by on fruit and bread and cold, dry cereal out of the box. She came with eggs and milk and bacon.

By the time he'd put away three eggs, half a dozen strips of bacon, four pieces of bread that she toasted by holding them on a long fork over the burner on the stove, complete with some of Annette's homemade strawberry jam, his stomach thought he'd died and gone to heaven.

He couldn't have suppressed the sigh of contentment once he finished even if he'd tried. Hank slid her head onto his knee and looked hopefully for a scrap. There weren't any. He scratched her ears.

"Sorry, old girl. It was too good."

Jill smiled. "Thank you."

He looked up and met her gaze. Then he hauled himself to his feet and started toward the door. "Better get goin'," he said. "Thanks for breakfast. And for...you know...bothering." He set his hat on his head and opened the door.

"Can I come?" Jill said. "Just for today," she added even as the word *no* was forming on his lips.

He hesitated, then nodded. "For today," he agreed.

After all, he reasoned, he could hardly say no when she'd done so much for him. Besides, she was leaving. For good.

Pretty soon memories would be the only thing he had.

Once, when he and Keith had been in Australia doing a movie, Luke had had the opportunity to spend the last evening he was there in a bar talking to an old Aborigine who had had a minor role in the film. The talk had ranged far and wide, covering the virtues of American versus Australian-rules football, the best points of American versus Australian saddles. And, of course, they'd spent considerable time debating—and sampling—a multitude of American and Australian beers.

But what stuck in Luke's mind now, five years later, was something the Australian had said about time. There was ordinary time, he'd told Luke, and there was ceremonial time. Dream time. A time that existed on another plane of reality altogether.

Then, muzzy-headed with beer and the fatigue that accompanied the end of shoot, Luke had only had a vague sort of grasp of what he was talking about. It made a lot more sense to him as he spent this day with Jill. He didn't know if the Aborigine would agree that what they were sharing that day was dream time or not, but as far as Luke was concerned, it qualified.

The day was clear and cool when they set out. First they fed the horses, then saddled up two of them and headed out so that Jill could show Luke the reluctant cows she'd met the day before. Then he showed her how to convince them to move and left her to it.

"Aren't you going to help?" she asked him.

"If you need it."

She got a small, determined smile on her face. Then she urged her horse forward. "Come on, cows," she said. "Move it."

Eventually they moved. She did surprisingly well. He smiled his approval. She smiled back. The day got a little warmer.

They made a circle to see to the cattle that she hadn't had a chance to check on the day before. Luke found one logy calf that he wanted to keep an eye on, so he drove it and its mother down to a lower pasture, the one where the steer that had been involved in his downfall still stood.

"This is the infirmary," Jill guessed.

"In a manner of speaking."

Jill shook her head and looked at him with a mixture of chagrin and pity. Then she rode up close and peered into his blackened eyes.

"They do give you a certain *je ne sais quoi,*" she told him, with only the barest twitch of her lips.

"It's nice to know a woman who can defend herself," Luke replied soberly.

And once more they smiled, and the day warmed even more. If Luke sensed the danger in those smiles or in the warm feelings growing between them, he ignored it. He just soaked up the impressions and the memories, willing to let the present take care of itself.

Dream time.

Yes, that's what it was.

It could have been meteorological conditions, or it could have been the increasing heat between them, but at that moment there was a white flash, followed by a loud peal of thunder. Huge clouds rumbled over the mountains and rain started pouring down.

Brief thunderstorms were frequent in the late afternoon during the summer months. But this one was a gully-washer, with thunder rumbling, lightning streaking and rain coming down in buckets.

"Come on," Luke shouted, touching his heels to his horse. "We're close to the cabin. Let's go."

Of course, they were drenched by the time they got there. And if it was possible to be any wetter, they got that way by the time they unsaddled and turned out the horses. Then, laughing and gasping, they ran across the clearing and stumbled up the steps and into the cabin. Luke slammed the door and fell back against it.

In front of him, Jill stood still, her jeans and shirt plastered against her skin, outlining her willowy curves. She turned and he saw her lips trembling. Her teeth chattered.

"Are you cold?" he asked her. He was burning himself, hotter now than he had been all day.

"No, uh . . . yes," she said, crossing her arms and rubbing her hands against her soaked sleeves.

"You'd . . . better get out of those clothes."

Their eyes met. Everything that had been growing all day—all week—hell, forever, as far as Luke was concerned—seemed suddenly too strong to deny.

Dream time.

Just today. He wouldn't ask for more than today.

"Jill?" His voice was ragged. He swallowed hard. "Take them off."

Her gaze dropped. She lifted her hands, and her fingers began to fumble with the buttons of her shirt, but they trembled and she made little progress.

"Let me?"

Her hands fell away. She looked up again, and everything he'd ever wanted to see in her eyes was there. More
than he deserved to see. More than he could accept. But
he couldn't look away. Not now. Not today.

"Just once," he whispered.

She tipped her head. "What?"

He gave his a little shake. "Nothing." He laid his
hands against her breasts and began to work the buttons
of her shirt. "If you want to say no, say it now."

A faint smile lit her face. "I'm not going to say no,
Luke." And then she raised her own hands and began to
undo his shirt as well.

Her fingers brushing against his chest made him tremble. Her breath against his lips made his knees shake. Her
mouth tracing the line of his jaw made him insane. He
practically tore her shirt getting those buttons undone.
But even when he got that done, it still clung wetly to her
skin and he nearly had to peel it off her. He made quicker
work of her bra, then bent his head and kissed the tip of
each uplifted breast.

"Luke!" She shivered at the touch of his lips, which
only made him want to kiss her more. And more.

Her hands moved to drag his shirt from his shoulders,
and he stepped back long enough to allow her that, then
wrapped his arms around her and hauled her close. It was
good. Hell, it was wonderful.

It wasn't enough. Soggy denim stood between them
and ecstasy. He moved impatiently to unfasten her jeans,
even as she was doing the same to his. The wetness of the
material prolonged the agony, yet somehow made the feel
of her naked skin against his, when it finally happened,
all that much better.

There were still boots. Luke didn't want to deal with boots. He wanted Jill now, all of her. But Jill had other ideas.

"Wait," she said. And she knelt in front of him, encouraging him to lift first one foot, then the other, so that she could tug off his boots. He did, bracing himself by holding onto her shoulders. His eyes fastened on her naked back, her curly, damp hair. He felt a surge of desire so strong it rocked him. And then she had his last boot off, had snaked his jeans away, too, and finally he was free.

Free to draw her down onto the bed and do the same to her, tugging her jeans and panties down her hips, then wiggling her free of both them and her boots so that she lay naked before him. Dream time. Heaven help him, yes.

She raised her arms to him, inviting him, and there wasn't the faintest possibility that he'd be able to say no. He'd lost whatever chance he had long before they'd started on each other's buttons, no matter what he said.

In dream time there was no past, there was no future, there was only now. And now was what Luke needed. The past hurt too much. The future was out of his reach. It didn't matter. For the moment he had everything.

He had Jill.

He lowered himself onto her, his hands stroking her soft damp skin, tangling in the wet curls of her hair. His lips brushed against her forehead, then nibbled at her brows, kissed her nose, then fastened at last on her mouth.

He intended to go slow, to savor, to prolong the joy and the excitement. But his will didn't get its way. The eager movement of Jill's body beneath his undid all his best intentions. It teased him and it coaxed him, and he was lost.

When her hands found him to bring him inside her, he had no power to resist. Nothing in him, not even his mind, at this point, wanted to resist. He only wanted her.

Dream time.

Yes, that's what it was. The one time when all was right with the world, when he was home and warm and safe and loved. When he was one with the woman who had somehow, from the first time he'd seen her, seemed an elemental part of his existence.

He didn't think about reality, didn't focus for once on the thousand things, large and small, that would prevent such a union. He couldn't. He was a part of it, consumed by it, wholly centered on Jill, on loving her the way she ought to be loved.

Just once.

And he did. He could see it in her face as she tossed her head from side to side. He could feel it in the clutch of her fingers against his back. He could savor it in the swift clench of her body around him, in the lift of her hips, in the press of her knees against his hips and, finally, in the soft groan of his name as she touched her lips to his.

It was this last gentle whisper that shattered him. All vestiges of control deserted him. He was lost. He was loved.

Dream time. His time. Her time.

He felt her hand stroke his hair, then move down to feather lightly along his back. She pressed a kiss to his shoulder, then another to his jaw. He lifted his head and looked down at her. She smiled. It was a soft smile, a gentle smile, a loving smile. She lifted her other hand and laid it lightly on the side of his face.

"I love you," she whispered softly.

Dream time was over. Well over.

He rolled away from her, onto his back, and folded his arms beneath his head.

"When are you going back to California—or is it New York?" he asked. He didn't look at her. He tried to keep his voice neutral, to keep all the emotions he felt roiling inside him shut out. He opened his eyes, but he looked at the rough-hewn wooden ceiling; he didn't look at her.

She didn't answer at once. She shifted on the bed. He could almost feel her withdrawing, regrouping, then preparing to mount another attack.

Don't, he wanted to beg her. *It won't help. It won't do either of us any good at all.*

"Actually," she said at last and with just the tiniest edge to her voice, "it's Los Angeles this time. It's a magazine assignment."

"Another movie star?"

She nodded. "Damon Hunter."

Luke knew Damon Hunter vaguely. They had met at several parties. Keith had never done a picture with him, but often the roles Keith hadn't taken, Damon had. Now Damon was getting roles that once would have been Keith's. Would he get Keith's girlfriend, too?

Behind his head, Luke's fingers tightened into fists. Consciously he worked at relaxing them, and telling himself he didn't care if Damon did, telling himself that her words of love didn't mean anything.

"You'll like that," he said with as much indifference as he could manage. "It's right up your alley."

"What's that mean?" He could hear her trying to keep her voice level.

"The movie-star bit." His mouth twisted cynically. "Another Keith."

"There will never be another Keith," she said simply. "But yes, I'll enjoy it. I like doing interviews. I like people. I like finding out what makes them tick."

"Is that what you've been doing with me?"

Her mouth pulled tight for a moment. "You know it's not."

"Yeah." He did, but he didn't really want to deal with it even now. "What's so interesting about movie stars?"

Jill shrugged. "The fame angle, I guess. Fame puts tremendous burdens on people. Regular people tend to think it makes the famous ones different, but it doesn't. They still want happiness and love and good health, just like the rest of us."

"And they have no more chance than we do of getting it," Luke said. "Take Keith."

"Keith loved his life," Jill said firmly. "He wouldn't have changed it. He wouldn't have done anything differently."

"He would have liked to have lived."

"Of course. But he made his own life, lived it on his own terms. Even when it was hard, he never ran away from it," she added. "And he never second-guessed himself."

"He never had time."

"Some of us have too much time."

"I wish I didn't," Luke muttered.

"Come back to L.A. with me. Go see Carl. I told you he wants you for a movie he's going to be doing."

"With who? Damon Hunter?"

"I don't know. It could be."

"No way." Luke shook his head adamantly.

"So what are you going to do? Sit up here on this mountain and wallow in your misery for the rest of your life? I thought you had more guts than that."

He looked at her, stung. "Damn it, what do you want me to do?"

"I want you to say that what happened to Keith was a terrible thing, but that you're not going to let it be the end of your life, too. I want you to come back and go to work again, pick up your life." She faced him squarely, her gray eyes imploring him, challenging him. "I want," she said softly, "for you to admit you love me, too."

Their eyes met. He saw urgency in hers, and support and something more.

Love? Promise? Faith in a future that he hadn't let himself believe in for years?

He didn't know. He didn't try to figure it out. He was afraid to.

Jill was right; he didn't have the guts. He could ride wild horses, jump off cliffs, wreck cars and walk away without a qualm. He couldn't do this.

As far as he was concerned, he had no right to the happiness that loving Jill would bring him.

"Luke?"

Slowly he let out a long breath, then shook his head. "I can't."

Nine

She left that evening after the weather cleared.

She didn't argue with him. She didn't berate him or harangue him. She didn't have to. He could see it in her eyes.

When he said, "I can't," the light simply went out of them. The color in her cheeks seemed to fade. Her mouth pressed into a thin line—not a hard line, just a sad one. She let out a slow breath, then turned away, dressing slowly, keeping her back to him, as if by doing so she could pretend he wasn't there.

He dressed, too, also without speaking. There wasn't really anything else to say until he stuffed his feet into his boots. Then he said, "I'll saddle your horse."

She nodded, her back still turned.

He let himself out into the cool evening air. It was that fresh, after-the-storm weather that washed the world clean and made everything look bright and new.

Luke didn't *feel* new. He felt a hundred years old. He moved as if he were that old, too. He knew it was prolonging the inevitable. He knew he was a fool. He ought to be running to saddle her horse and get her on her way.

But everything he did seemed in slow motion. He felt numb. He caught her horse and even debated briefly about whether he ought to ride down with her. He decided against it.

He wanted it over, didn't he?

He got the horse saddled and bridled, then led it back to the cabin. Jill was waiting on the porch.

She had the clothes she'd brought packed in her saddlebags. He took them from her and slung them over the back of the horse and tied them on. Then he handed her the reins.

They faced each other. The wind lifted her hair, trailing strands across her cheek. Unconsciously she tucked them back behind her ear. Overhead Luke could hear a jay scolding. He could hear his own breath whistling lightly between barely parted lips.

He started to move them, to force "goodbye" past them with all the indifference he could manage.

But before he could, she took a step toward him. She lifted her hand and brushed light fingers over his battered forehead, then let them linger for just a moment on his cheek.

He held himself rigid. Then she leaned forward. Her lips brushed a fleeting kiss across his and just as quickly were gone again.

But not so quickly that his fists didn't clench at his sides. Not so quickly that he didn't have all he could do not to reach for her, not to grab her and hang on, not to take the kiss he really wanted.

He held himself tightly in check, stiff as a fence post, not even breathing, as she gave him one last, wistful smile. Then she turned and swung up into the saddle.

"Goodbye, Luke," she whispered.

And was it only the breeze or did he hear the whispered words *I love you,* as she rode away?

He didn't stay to watch her leave.

As she rode off, he turned and strode toward the shed. He moved quickly, grabbing his own saddle and tack, then whistling for his horses. He saddled the buckskin, his movements swift and jerky.

The horse whinnied and shifted, aware of Luke's agitation, unaware of what was causing it, yet becoming agitated himself as Luke swung into the saddle and kicked him into a trot up the mountainside.

He was a snuffy horse, big and strong and hard to control. Exactly the challenge Luke needed now. He would have liked to have galloped flat out. Too bad he had more sense. Otherwise he could have broken his fool neck and been done with all the pain. But like as not he'd have broken the horse's, too, so he didn't. He just rode. And rode. And rode.

He didn't let himself think about Jill riding down the mountain. He didn't let himself imagine her saying goodbye to Jimmy and Annette. He didn't envision her giving Jimmy, Jr. a bear hug and dropping a gentle kiss on baby Julie's head. He turned his mind away from the thought of her getting into her little red rental car and driving out onto the highway, heading for the airport, heading for the plane that would take her to Denver and then to Los Angeles.

Or he tried to stop thinking about her, anyway.

The ground was wet from all the rain. The branches that slapped him as he rode showered him again and again. And when he could ride no longer, he stopped by the trees where he and Keith had sat that autumn day almost two years ago.

He thought about things he wished he could change. He thought about Keith. He thought about Jill. He scrubbed at his eyes with the back of his hand. Damn branches, shaking water down that way.

His horse shifted beneath him. He patted her neck. "Let's go then," he said, and tugged his hat down and rode west, down the mountain, into one of God's most spectacular sunsets.

If there was an irony to the way his life was turning out, he wasn't in the mood to appreciate it.

He'd lived in the cabin by himself for more than a year. It had never really bothered him before.

It was lonely now. He told himself that was nonsense. Mere days of Jill's presence could hardly have made that much difference.

But when he lit the lamp, the first sight that met his eyes was the bed where they'd made love. The sleeping bag was still rumpled. On the pillow, close together, were the depressions where two heads had lain. Muttering under his breath, Luke plumped the pillow and shook out the sleeping bag, then spread it out again.

There. Now it was as if she'd never been here.

Except there was a pile of paper sitting on the table.

He frowned. What the . . . ?

He crossed the room and picked it up, and knew even as he did so exactly what he would find.

Luke's fingers clenched around the manuscript, then he dropped it and turned away. He didn't want to read it, damn it. She knew that.

So why had she...?

He muttered an expletive under his breath and banged back outside to sit on the steps. But there was no relief. It was there, taunting him, beckoning to him. He swatted a deerfly, then another. Slapping and muttering more, he banged back inside again.

And saw the manuscript.

He wasn't going to read it. He wasn't! His eyes hurt. His face was still swollen. Even if he wanted to—which he didn't—he was in no shape to read.

So he ignored it. He picked up the rope he'd been braiding before Jill had invaded his life. It seemed like aeons ago. He needed to get back to it, needed to get his bearings. He dropped down on the bed, tugged off his boots, stretched out, leaned against the wall and started to work once more on the rope.

But he could see the manuscript out of the corner of his eye even when he concentrated on the rope.

He looked away.

What had Jill used of what he'd given her? he wondered. Which, if any, of his stories had she told? What did she say about his friendship with Keith? What, if anything, had she said about what had existed between the three of them?

Damn it, nothing had existed.

She had said that, hadn't she?

He turned and looked at the manuscript, then turned away again and tried to concentrate on the rope. Usually he could braid automatically. Tonight he got knots. He cursed, started again, turned his head and looked at the manuscript once more.

Was Keith there between those pages? The Keith he remembered?

Was the Keith he remembered the same man that she knew?

"Aw, hell." He tossed the rope aside and stood up, got the manuscript and sat down with it on the bunk.

He shut his eyes. His fists, resting atop the paper, tightened briefly. Then he drew a breath, opened his eyes and moved his hands away.

He started to read.

He didn't really know what he expected. Something dry and two-dimensional, perhaps. Something sad and schmaltzy, maybe. Certainly a mere facsimile of the vital, vibrant man Keith Mallory had been.

It wasn't what he got. What he got was the Keith he knew and loved—his best friend of all time—and another Keith—*many* other Keiths—that he had never known at all.

From the start Luke and Keith had taken each other at face value. They had never poked and probed into each other's past. Keith had known of Luke's brothers. He had known Luke's parents were dead.

But Luke had never entertained him with stories of his growing-up years. He had never confessed the fear and pain he'd felt when his mother had died, when he was only five. He had never admitted the desperation, the panic he'd felt at sixteen when his father had been killed in a riding accident. He'd never talked about his subsequent scrapes and brushes with "authority," nor about the times his older brother had had to bail him out. He had certainly never told Keith about feeling responsible for his brother's marriage going wrong. What was past was past. He didn't talk about it.

And Keith had never really talked about his past, either.

So Luke had never known about Keith's parents. Keith had never mentioned them. Not to him, anyway.

But they were here because Jill knew about them. Probably, Luke realized, Keith hadn't opened up to her, either. Not at first. But Jill had persisted. She'd asked. She'd cared. Luke could see that right away. This was no dry, objective study. This was a labor of love.

And what she hadn't learned from Keith, she'd learned after his death, by talking to those who'd known him as a child. She couldn't ask his mother, because she'd died when Keith was twenty-two.

But she had found his father, a hard-edged Los Angeles businessman with little time for anyone, a man who was in fact reluctant to admit that film idol Keith Mallory was his son.

"He lived a frivolous life," Ronald Mallory had told Jill in the brief interview he'd granted her.

But from the way Jill showed Keith—and the way Luke remembered him—his life was anything but frivolous. It was a celebration.

But it was a celebration, Luke discovered, that had grown out of confronting pain and moving beyond it. As he read of Keith's relationship with his parents, he understood him far better than he had when he was living with him day by day.

He met Keith the child, bright, yet shy, and almost pathetically eager to please. He saw Keith the only son, seeking his father's approval desperately, yet willing to fight that father whenever he felt his mother was threatened.

And threatened she'd apparently been—though that was something else Keith had never told Luke.

Luke was shaken by what he read. The Keith he'd known had seemed golden, blessed, the possessor of talent, looks, brains and charm. He had trouble imagining at first a Keith for whom things had sometimes been uncertain, bleak and even frightening.

But the more he read, the more it made sense. It clarified Keith's sometimes-desperate competitiveness. It made his sheer exuberance and childlike delight at simple joys much more understandable. It made his gentleness with women and children far clearer.

It made Luke pause for thought.

He thought he'd made pretty vast changes in his life with his move from rural Colorado to fast-lane L.A., but he saw that geography and life-style weren't the only sorts of changes a man could make.

He read on. He met Keith the brother. Another revelation. He'd never even known Keith had sisters. He had. Two of them, both younger.

Jill had found them. Maybe she'd even met them before Keith's death. Maybe Keith had shared them with her. In any case, both had related stories that showed Keith to be equally protective of them.

In subsequent chapters Luke met other Keiths—the schoolboy, the swimmer, the striver. Mischievous and competitive. Dogged and determined, yet always ready for a laugh. The coach's dream, the athlete who was always ready to go one better, to fight just a little harder, to take on one more challenge. These were Keiths he knew, and yet they, too, were clearer now.

And then there was the Keith who acted, the Keith who became all things in one man, who did whatever the script demanded. Luke knew him almost as well as he knew himself. But Jill had known him better. Better, probably, then Keith even knew himself.

Luke found the stories he'd told Jill. The catacombs story, the skateboard story, the ones that showed Keith off the set to be as zany and likable and charming as the scripts made him out to be in the roles he played.

They were exactly as he had told them—and yet, reading them, seeing them happening in his mind's eye as they had once happened in reality, Luke understood them better, too. They made him smile. They made his throat tighten and his eyes sting. He blinked a few times, then read on.

He met the Keith Jill knew.

The Keith he'd never known, for all that they had been best friends.

Jill's Keith was the man who'd stood behind the man the public met, the man who'd laughed and joked and roughnecked with Luke. This was the Keith who had lived with pain and uncertainty and fear. This was the Keith who knew his limitations all too well. Or feared he did.

He was afraid of marriage, Jill wrote. Luke stared at the words, astonished. He'd never heard Keith claim any such thing. But even as he read the words and doubted them, he sensed that they were true.

He remembered wondering over the almost two years Jill and Keith were an item why they didn't get married. He even remembered asking once or twice. Jokingly, of course. Not seriously. Certainly not as if he cared.

Both times Keith had brushed him off, had said something vague about doubting if Jill would have him, which at the time Luke had thought was the biggest crock in the world. But now, knowing what he knew, he supposed maybe Keith had meant what he'd said.

Certainly that was what he'd told Jill. His own parents' marriage had been so bad, he'd been terrified at the thought of trying it himself.

"You should have children," Jill wrote that she'd told him once when they were walking along the beach and a couple of little boys had nagged him into building a sand castle with them. He'd done it willingly, eagerly. "Don't you want children?" she had asked him.

Keith had said that he did. "A lot. I love kids," he'd told her. "They have such promise."

Luke could remember him saying that, too.

"I'd like to have children, too," Jill had told Keith wistfully. "With you," she'd added, in case he didn't get it.

"You mean marry me?" Keith had asked her. There had been what seemed an eternal pause, a pause long enough for Jill to wish she'd never made any hints at all, to wish that she were fifty feet underground or fifty states away, to regret her presumption a thousand times over.

And then he'd asked, "What if I'm like my old man?"

His hesitation hadn't had anything to do with her at all. She'd been amazed.

"You're not," she'd told him. But he'd looked doubtful. And finally she'd said, "I don't believe you are. Not for a minute." Then she'd looked him straight in the eyes and said, "I'm willing to risk it. I'm willing to do whatever it takes. Are you?"

And because he was Keith, and because he loved her, he'd said yes. He took the risk. He made up his mind to try.

That was the best part of Keith, Jill wrote at the very end of her book. *He was never afraid to put his hopes— his future—on the line.*

Keith Mallory died far too young. He died in an accident that needn't have happened, but he died in circumstances that he himself chose. He made his life, and himself, what he wanted them to be. He always tried to be the best Keith Mallory he could be. Ultimately, his legacy to us is not a list of films he made or the parts he played. His legacy is his life, the example he gave to those of us privileged to know him.

That night Luke had the dream again. They were bodysurfing, he and Keith. Jill was standing on the pier, watching, waving, smiling, pointing out the wave of the day. They caught it, the two of them. It swept them high and fast, then flung them over. They crashed, struggled, tangled, parted, reached. Their fingers touched just for a moment. An instant, no more.

It was the same, except the end. This time Keith made it to shore.

It was Luke who slipped away....

"What happened to your face?"

Luke sat bolt upright, stunned and shaking. He stared around wildly, trying to get his bearings, still drowning, floundering up to find Paco standing at the end of his bunk.

The boy was looking at him, concerned. "Somebody hit your face? That why you were yelling?"

Luke lifted a hand and touched his face gently, wincing. He scowled. "Wasn't yelling," he muttered. He eyed Paco narrowly through the swelling. "What the hell are you doing here?"

"Was so yelling," Paco said stoutly. "Thought somebody was killin' you. It's why I came in. Jill sent me," he added.

Luke's head snapped up. "What?"

Paco shrugged narrow shoulders. "She said you needed help. She said to come."

"Well, you can just damn well go home again!" Luke hauled himself to his feet. The manuscript, which had been lying on his lap, cascaded to the floor, scattering papers all over. "Damn."

"What's that?" Paco said, bending to start picking all of it up.

"Jill's book."

The boy's eyes widened. "The one about Keith? Can I read it?"

"I don't know, can you?" Luke started to duck down to help Paco pick up papers, but his head hurt when he bent over. He straightened up again, grimacing.

Paco didn't notice. "I can try," he said eagerly as he straightened the pages. "Will you help me with the words I don't know?"

"No." Luke turned away, raking a hand through his hair, then stopped and sighted. "Oh, hell, I guess."

Paco beamed. "Thanks. I'll finish picking this up while you make coffee. Then we can get to work. An' tonight I can read."

"I don't need—" *Any help,* Luke started to say, but he didn't finish, because the fact of the matter was, he did. Jill, damn her, was right. She knew him, like she'd known Keith, even better than he knew himself.

Until the swelling in his face went down, until he could see better, he *did* need someone. Even someone as little as Paco. Well, fine. He'd agree. As long as it wasn't her.

"Yeah, awright. Just lemme get some coffee and we'll go."

He turned his back on the boy and the manuscript, grabbing the pot and heading out the door. When he got back, having fetched the water and dunked his head in the creek, Paco was reading the book. He didn't even look up.

Luke made the coffee, then changed his shirt, dragged a comb through his hair and sort of made up his bunk. By the time he finished, the coffee was ready. He poured himself a mug, then glanced at Paco, still reading.

"Want some?" he asked.

Paco didn't even look up. Obviously Jill had captured another reader. Luke pulled a wry face and took a long, scalding swallow from the mug.

"She's gone then?" he asked, without even realizing he was going to.

"Huh?" Paco looked up as if he were coming back from a long way away, then realized what Luke was asking him. "Oh, Jill? Yeah, she left last night."

That surprised him. She'd only left him last night. "Planes go out that late now?"

Paco shook his head. "She drove to Albuquerque." He said this last as if it ought to have been obvious and bent his head over the book once more.

Luke supposed it was if he gave it any thought. She could hardly want to hang around. Hell, he couldn't blame her. He finished off his coffee and clanked the mug down into the dishpan. "Come on. Let's get going."

"Can't I just finish the first—"

"Later." And Luke strode out the door and clumped down the steps without looking back. Behind him he could hear Paco scrambling to catch up.

This morning's weather was clear and cool and fresh after yesterday afternoon's torrential downpour. The world looked bright and new. The first day of the rest of his life, as the cliché went....

The first day of the rest of his life without Jill.

It was what he wanted, damn it. It was what he deserved, wasn't it?

"'S a good book, I think," Paco was saying seriously as he rode up alongside. "So far, anyhow. I'm only on, like, page 20, 'cause you wouldn't let me go any further."

"You said you came to work."

"Yeah, well, I am," Paco replied. "But I like Jill's book. Did you like it, Luke?"

Luke grunted and touched his heels to his horse.

"I didn't know Keith had two sisters like I got," Paco went on, keeping up. "You didn't tell me that," he added accusingly.

"I didn't know."

"How come?"

Luke shrugged irritably. "Never came up. Come on. See those cows down there in that willow thicket? Let's move 'em out."

The creek was still running high from the storm and Luke's horse stumbled, getting its footing as he maneuvered in close and began urging a bunch of cows back up the mountain. Paco's tongue poked out from between the thin line of his lips as he concentrated on doing the same. The cows moved with their customary reluctance, ambling up the slope, stopping to swat at flies, and then, when Luke whooped them on, finally moving again. He was willing to bet they'd be right back down there tomorrow.

The second day of the rest of his life.

He wheeled his horse around. "I'm going to look over in the meadow beyond the ridge, see if I can find the bull. You ride this bunch on up, okay?"

"By myself?" Paco looked doubtful and eager at the same time.

"If you think you can do it."

Paco's chin came up. "'Course I can do it."

Luke allowed himself a smile. "Good. When you've got 'em up, ride along that fence above the rise. I'll meet you by the pines near the river."

Paco nodded. "Sure. I brought some lunch in my saddlebags. My mom made us sandwiches an' sent apples, an' Annette stuck in a whole bunch of brownies and some cherry pie. We can eat up there, 'kay?"

Luke tugged on the brim of his hat. "Right. See you then."

It wasn't that he didn't want to spend time with Paco, it was just that right now it was too much. He was still raw from Jill, still trying to shake off a night spent reading about Keith—a Keith so real and so vital that it was inconceivable to think that he was dead.

But he was dead.

And for all that she had created a work of art in her manuscript, Jill's book couldn't change that.

He found the bull, his foot wedged between some rocks where the creek had overflowed. He was snorting and tugging and should have been happy when Luke showed up to get him out. Of course, if he was, he was in no mood to express his appreciation. In fact, he barely missed nailing Luke's ribs where they had finally begun feeling better.

"Ingrate," Luke called when the animal, freed finally, snorted and tossed his head, then trotted away. But the bull was easier to deal with than Paco talking incessantly about Keith. Luke lifted his hat and shoved a weary hand through sweat-dampened hair, then he settled his hat back on his head, turned his horse and started up the mountain.

Paco was already there, sitting by the stand of pines near the storm-swollen river. He was eating an apple and he had the rest of the food laid out on a flat rock, but he bounced to his feet when he saw Luke coming. "I got all the cows up," he announced. "An' I checked the fence. It's fine. An' the gate's shut."

Luke swung down off his horse. "Thanks." He ruffled a hand through Paco's short, dark hair. "You did good."

Paco grinned and grabbed some of the food. "Mom packed ham and cheese and peanut butter and jelly. Which do you want?"

Luke settled under the tree with a ham-and-cheese sandwich, an apple and two pieces of the cherry pie that Annette had made. Paco ate his apple and swung from the branches and asked Luke if Keith had ever swung out of trees the way Tarzan did. Then he ate a peanut-butter sandwich and balanced along the dead logs, hopping from one to another, his arms outstretched, and asked if Keith had ever tried tightrope walking. After he'd finished, he helped himself to the brownies and, with one in each hand and the remains of another in his mouth, he went to walk along the edge of the steep bluff above the surging river.

"Did Keith ever—"

"Get back from there," Luke snapped at him. But it was too late.

He'd barely spoken when Paco said, "Hey!" and tumbled over the edge of the bluff into the rampaging water below.

"Paco!" Luke shot to his feet, scrambling over a fallen log, tripping on a rock, lurching to stand at the crumbled edge of the bluff in time to see Paco's dark head disappear as he was carried downstream by the force of the water. "Paco!"

He stopped to think only one thing: *Paco couldn't swim.* Then he yanked off his boots and flung himself in. The icy, churning water closed over his head, dashing him hard against the rocks. He fought his way to the surface, scanning the river for any sign of the boy.

"Paco!" He screamed the boy's name and was rewarded by the briefest flick of an arm lifted in a wave— and then it was gone again.

He struck out for where it had been, swimming as desperately as he ever had, shoving himself away from rocks he scraped over, fighting for every bit of headway he could make.

"Try for the bank," he yelled. "Grab on to something!" But the sound of the river pouring over rocks swallowed his words, and he knew that chances were Paco never heard them.

Every few seconds he caught sight of the boy—an arm, his dark hair, once only a hand—and the terror he knew at the thought of Paco being pulled down, being caught, trapped the way Keith had been, went like a shaft right through him.

"Please, God, no!" he cried.

And then, thank God—for no one else could have done anything—Paco caught on to the face of a rock outcrop. His grip was tenuous as he fought the current. Luke could see him looking back, his face white and his dark eyes wide with panic.

"Hang on," he yelled.

And Paco did, for as long as he could. Then, right before Luke had him, just as his fingers touched him, Paco reached for him, lost his purchase on the rock and slipped away.

"No! Damn it! No!"

It was the nightmare come to life. The panic of losing Keith all over again.

Luke kicked and plunged back into the current, pushing himself, reaching . . . reaching . . . touching . . . grabbing—*a hand.*

He jerked it, pulled as hard as he could, sank under, fought his way up with one hand and his feet, never letting go of those small fingers with the other. *Come on. Come on.* And then the hand fastened hard on his, clawed its way up his arm and—

"Got you!" Luke said it through a mouthful of water, looked into Paco's terrified face and did his best to grin. They weren't through it yet. Not nearly.

The current had them again, sweeping them ever downward. The river had widened here, making it less fearsome in one respect, more so in another. There was less chance of them getting caught as Keith had between rocks, but it was farther to the safety of the shore.

"Hang onto my neck," he told Paco. "Don't fight it."

Paco's teeth were chattering. His fingers bit into Luke's arms, then got a stranglehold on his neck, almost choking him.

"Go easy," Luke said, and he could feel Paco trying, but he knew it wasn't easy. Not for either of them. Slowly he fought his way toward the bank, and at last, he caught onto a rock.

"Here. Let go of me. Grab on here."

"No! I can't! I need—"

"Do it!" Luke commanded. He couldn't hang on much longer. The weight of the boy was pulling him back into the current. "Come on. Grab! Now!"

He reached back and pried the boy's fingers loose, put them on the rock. Paco clung to it, terrified.

"Pull yourself up."

"I c-can't." His teeth were chattering so badly he could hardly talk.

"You can," Luke insisted through his own clenched teeth. "You've got to. Keith would."

Paco looked over his shoulder. Their eyes met.

"Do it."

He gave the boy a shove with all the strength he had left. Paco made it up onto the rock.

It was the last thing Luke saw before the water closed over his head and he was swept away.

Ten

It was what he'd wanted, wasn't it?

To give up.

To let go.

To die . . . like Keith had.

He hadn't saved Keith, but he had saved Paco. The boy was tired, scared, shaken to the core, but he was safe. He would make himself do now whatever he thought Keith would do.

He'd make it.

Luke didn't have to.

He was tired, god-awful tired. He'd been tired so long he couldn't remember ever not being tired. The water didn't seem so cold now. Nor so frightening. It seemed almost friendly, sweeping him along, pulling him down.

It would be so easy to stop fighting it, to quit.

To die.

He'd toyed with death often enough over the past few years that his life no longer passed before his eyes. He didn't see the things he'd done, the places he'd been. He'd seen them all before.

He saw instead the things he'd miss.

His mind filled with scenes of sunsets and sunrises, roundups and brandings, snowfalls and storms—all the things he loved that he'd never see again.

Was that what every man saw in his last moments?

Was that what Keith had seen?

Had Keith seen Jill?

Luke was seeing her now. His mind cleared of everything but the sight of her.

There was no river, no rocks, no roiling water. There was only Jill looking at him, a sad, wistful half smile on her face. He remembered that look, that smile. He'd seen them on her face the first time they'd made love, and the second.

He'd seen them again after she'd asked him to come with her, after he'd said, "I can't."

He hadn't understood what he was seeing then. Now he did. It was his future slipping away from him. The future he would miss if he quit.

Keith never quit.

Luke remembered his bloody, scraped fingertips. No, Keith hadn't quit. He'd fought with everything that was in him for his life, for his future, for his dreams.

"We're two of a kind," he remembered Keith saying once. He could almost feel Keith with him now, challenging him. *Go for it, man.*

Two of a kind?

God, yes!

The resolution he hadn't thought he had took hold, galvanizing him.

Yes! He owed it to Keith to keep fighting. He owed it to Paco. He owed it to Noah, who'd told him so. He owed it to Jill, who'd believed in him. *He owed it to himself*. It was a strange thought, almost foreign. He'd denied it so long. He didn't deny it now.

He wanted the future. He wanted the hope, the dreams, the promise.

He wanted to share them with Jill.

He started struggling again, fighting his way up, looking desperately for the bank, for a rock, for anything to hang onto. Please God, he didn't want to die!

White water surged over him. He got a mouthful, then another . . . and another.

Jill!

He fought upward, struggled toward the bank, his lungs searing, his arms leaden, his body a sodden log.

Jill! I'm coming! Help me, Jill!

He used every ounce of strength he had, fighting and pushing until at last his fingers scrabbled against rock. He hauled himself up, shaking, gasping, then fell headlong against the cold, wet stone. His heart thundered and his head still pounded with the sound of the river inches away.

He was out. He was alive.

He had a future.

With Jill?

He prayed to God that he hadn't left it too late.

She was nowhere to be found.

She was gone. Not just gone from Colorado. Of course, he knew that. He knew she'd gone to L.A.

He left the next morning—hired Doug, another Sutter, to help out, accepted gratefully Cy's offer as well and caught the next plane to L.A. Urgent business, he told

Annette and Jimmy. He didn't tell them what. A man had his pride, after all.

But she wasn't in L.A.

Or maybe she was, but he couldn't find her.

He used every connection he could think of to find out where the hotshot young actor Damon Hunter, the subject of her proposed interview, lived.

But when he got to Hunter's Malibu canyon hideaway, talked his way past first the gardener and then the maid and was finally allowed to see the movie star himself, she'd come and gone.

"She's a quick worker," Hunter told him with a grin.

"Was she going home from here? Did she say?"

Hunter shook his head. "She looked like she needed a vacation. She was pale, you know?"

Luke grunted. If she was, he'd probably made her that way. "Thanks," he said, and turned to go.

"She give you those shiners, man?" Hunter asked, still grinning.

Luke turned again, his teeth clenched. Hunter took a step back, holding up his hands as if to protect himself.

"Hey, man, I was only askin'. I just wouldn't want to get on the wrong side of anybody who could do that."

Luke was already on Jill's wrong side. But the shiners hadn't hurt nearly as badly as not being able to find her now did.

He called Annette and Jimmy to see how things were going, then told them he was flying to New York.

"Flying to New York? Now? One way? Gosh," Annette said, "I guess you really are rich."

Luke didn't feel very rich. He felt especially poor when he got there, went to the apartment building where she lived and found out she wasn't there, either, and no one would say where she was.

"You think I should tell you about my tenants, you got another think comin', fella," the building super said.

"I'm a friend."

"Ya don' look very friendly." The super studied Luke's face, which was still a mottled blend of purple, blue and ghastly green. "Ya can leave a message if ya want."

"I'll wait."

The man shrugged. "Suit yourself."

Luke waited. All day. All evening. Into the night. He sat on a small bench in the foyer and watched Jill's neighbors in the West Side, prewar building as they came and went. He waited in vain.

"Ya can't sit here all night," the super told him.

"You've got a 24-hour doorman," Luke said. "Why can't I?"

"Because I said so. Get a hotel room and come back in the morning."

"Will she be here in the morning?"

"Who knows?"

She didn't come back in the morning, nor in the afternoon, nor in the evening, nor at any time during the remainder of the week.

"Ya know what they say about gettin' a life?" the super said to Luke on the sixth day.

"Yeah." He didn't want to leave, but the super was right. And whether he wanted it anymore or not, he had a life. It was his ranch. His responsibilities. He couldn't depend on Jimmy and Doug and Cy indefinitely. He had to go back.

He scribbled his number on a piece of paper and held it out to the other man. "Listen. Will you call and tell me as soon as she comes home?"

"I can't do that."

"Please. All I want is a chance to talk to her."

"There's phones."

"She'd hang up on me. Please." Luke thrust out the paper once more.

The super hesitated. "How many days you been here? Six? Seven? You're some persistent fella, ain'tcha?"

"Some damn fool, actually. Will you?"

"Well..."

"Please." And this please was accompanied by a hundred-dollar bill.

The super grinned and scratched his head. "Well, when you put it that way..."

But when more than a month went by and he hadn't heard a word, he pretty much gave up on getting the call. He still phoned Carl every few days to find out if he'd heard anything and still got the same negative answer. But it was all he could think of doing.

It had taken all his courage to make that first call, and when he had, Carl hadn't been easy on him.

"Finished whining, have you? Stopped running?" he'd asked when he heard Luke's voice the first time.

It stung, but Luke knew he deserved it.

"Yeah, I am," he'd said. "I need to see Jill."

"Don't imagine she wants to see you."

"Did she say that?"

"Didn't have to. A guy only had to look at her. My God, man, don't you think she's been through enough?"

"I want to apologize. I want to..." He stopped. He couldn't tell Carl what he wanted. He couldn't tell anyone but Jill. And he intended to fly back out to New York or to L.A. or wherever he needed to in order to pick up her trail again once they'd gathered and shipped the cattle the first part of October. But that was two weeks away, and until then he had his hands full.

The range work all fell to Luke, but Jimmy was doing the paperwork now, and that helped. Doug had gone back to college at the end of August, though Cy still came out every day to lend a hand. They were coping, but the next two weeks would be hectic. And thank God for that. He spent most nights lying awake staring at the ceiling of the cabin, remembering Jill lying beside him. At least he was distracted from similar memories most of the days.

He was so distracted he didn't even connect when he came in for supper that night and Annette told him that a man named Eddie had called.

"That the guy with the Saler bull for sale?"

"I don't think so. He said he's from New York City and—" Annette wrinkled her nose in puzzlement "—to tell you that your pigeon had landed."

"Boy, you didn't waste no time," Eddie, the super, said when Luke walked into the foyer of Jill's apartment building early the next morning. He was grinning from ear to ear. "You're looking' better. No more bruises."

Not on the outside, anyway. Luke had sat up all night on the red-eye flight, trying to think about what he would say, and now his mind was blank. "Is she still up there?"

"Less she went out the fire escape. Came in yesterday afternoon and hasn't been out yet."

Luke headed toward the elevator. "Thanks."

"Hey, I gotta tell her you're coming." The super gestured toward the in-house phone.

Luke looked at him imploringly. "Please." He started to dig into his pocket, but the super waved him on.

"Just you be nice to her or it'll be my job."

The question was would *she* be nice to *him?* Luke knew he had no right to expect it. If she shut the door in his face it would be no more than he deserved. He just hoped he could get the toe of his boot in before she did so.

She lived on the fifteenth floor. The elevator had fancy inlaid wood in the paneling. The foyer outside the six apartments was carpeted with thick, rose-colored plush to muffle sound. Still Luke could hear himself breathing, could hear his heart pounding. He wiped damp palms on his jeans, shut his eyes briefly, then opened them again and knocked on the door.

The door jerked open. "Cara, I'm fine, really, I—" Jill stopped dead. What little color there was in her cheeks drained totally away.

Luke managed what he hoped was a smile. "Hi."

He saw her swallow. Her fingers tightened into a fist. "Luke."

"Can I come in?"

She hesitated a moment, then stepped back and let him in. Then she shut the door, skirted quickly around him and led the way into a sun-drenched room with a view of the park. It was a warm room filled with furniture that wouldn't have looked out of place back in Colorado.

He noticed for the first time that she wasn't dressed— not in street clothes, anyway. She wore a robe, tied loosely around her middle, and her long hair hung down her back.

"Are you sick?" he demanded.

She turned and faced him, shaking her head. Her fingers gripped the back of an armchair so tightly that her knuckles were white. "I'm fine."

"You thought I was somebody else," he said. "Somebody who was worried about you."

She shrugged. "My neighbor across the way, Cara. She knew I came home last night and she— Never mind about me. What are you doing here?"

He wondered where to start. "I read your book," he said at last.

"Oh?" He could hear the caution in her voice, the wariness that she had every right to feel.

"It was great. I never ... I never knew. About Keith, I mean, about his parents. He never said. He never told me any of it."

Jill lifted her shoulders. "I'm not surprised," she said softly. "I think I was the only one he ever told. I debated for a long time about putting it in the book. I wondered if it was disloyal."

"It's not. It makes him clear. It makes him whole. It makes sense out of a lot of things that I never really understood."

"Good." Their eyes met for a moment, then she looked away.

She might have been on vacation, but he thought she still looked tired. There were dark circles under her eyes and she looked as if she'd lost weight. She twisted her hands together, then glanced toward the door.

"Thank you for telling me." *And now, goodbye.* He could hear the words even if she didn't actually say them.

"That's not all," he said quickly. "It ... it made me think. What you said ... about Keith always trying to be the best Keith he could. That was true. He was. And he is ..." he hesitated a second, then plunged on, "an example. But you know—" and here he managed a wry smile "—I've got a hell of a long way to go." He looked straight at her and gave her his heart. "I could use your help."

She didn't reply. She stood staring at him, absolutely mute, and he went on desperately, "I know I don't have any right to expect it. Reckon you have every reason to tell me to go to hell." He dug a toe of his boot into the rug underfoot, then slanted her a quick glance and saw her run her tongue over her lips.

"What sort of help?" she asked hollowly, when he'd almost given up hope that she'd ever speak again.

He ducked his head, unable to look at her straight on. He rubbed a hand against the back of his neck. "Love me," he said. It was barely more than a whisper. He didn't think she could have heard him, except he heard her suck in her breath.

"I need you to," he went on doggedly. "I know I said I didn't want this. I know I said I couldn't live with the guilt of having what should have been Keith's. But what you wrote—about Keith taking a chance on life, about him never quitting. Well, you were right. He hated quitters. I guess," he said, his mouth twisting in a ghost of a grin, "I didn't want him lookin' down at me and callin' me one."

"That's why, is it?" Jill said softly, but there was just the hint of a smile on her face.

Luke nodded. "That's why. And because I love you." And then he stared at her, stricken. "Oh, God in heaven, don't cry. Please don't."

But she was, and he stood there, dumb as a crutch, not having the faintest idea what to do to stop her.

He took a step toward her, then halted, but the tears kept on and he couldn't bear it. "Jeez, Jill, you gotta stop. Please. I'll leave. Look, I'll just get out and you won't have to see me ever again. I promise. I—" He turned and headed for the door.

"No!" She held out her arms to him, tears still rolling down her face. "No. Don't go. I never thought you'd come. Please don't go."

He didn't. He went instead straight into her arms. He put his arms around her as well, crushing her against him, savoring the sensation of her trembling body pressed against him, relishing the softness of her skin and the touch of her lips on his. He brushed his fingers through her hair and kissed away her tears.

"I don't want to make you cry," he murmured. "I've made your life miserable enough."

She shook her head, smiling at him, touching his cheek with her fingers, as if when he'd come, he'd brought the sun. And damned if the room didn't seem lighter now, but Luke figured it was on account of her smile.

"I never thought you'd come," she confessed again.

"I'm a hard-headed son-of-a-gun. Takes me awhile to smarten up. Nothing like almost losing your life to figure out what makes it worth saving."

She looked at him worriedly. "What do you mean?"

So he told her. She drew him down onto the sofa in the living room and he cuddled her next to him while he told her about reading the manuscript, about having it still echoing in his head when Paco had fallen in the river.

He told her about the struggle to get the boy, and he hurried his explanation along when he saw how worried she was that something dreadful had happened.

"But I got him out," he said. "I got sucked back in and I was ready to give up. Then I remembered Keith. And I remembered you...and suddenly the future started makin' a lot more sense."

"I'm glad," Jill whispered as she turned in his arms. "You don't know how glad."

He rested his forehead against hers and took a shaky breath. "You think maybe you could show me?"

She smiled. "I think maybe I could."

She did, and her loving was sweeter than he remembered. Her body was lusher than he remembered, even though she was willowy still. Her touch was gentle, her kisses achingly tender. And as he matched her, touch for touch, kiss for kiss, he found he matched her tears as well, and he didn't even flinch when she touched one with her thumb and brushed it softly away.

"I tried to find you," he told her afterward, when they lay in her bed curled in each other's arms. "I went to see Hunter in L.A. I came back here and bribed Eddie, the super. I called Carl so often he thought I was deranged."

"Did you?" She sounded delighted. "I had no idea." Her smile faded slightly. "After that last day I had no hopes left."

"Where did you go? After L.A., I mean?"

"A friend of mine has a place in the woods in British Columbia. I went there. I needed to put my head back together, to figure out how to get on with my life. I had things to cope with I hadn't counted on." She turned in his arms, looking away from him. He felt a moment's panic.

"Being alone, you mean?"

"No." She paused and looked back at him. "Having a child."

For a long moment her words held no meaning for him. A child? What child? He looked at her closely and, all at once, saw new meaning in the dark hollows under her eyes, in the tired, gaunt look on her face. He found new meaning in the slight differences he'd felt in her body when they'd made love.

"A child? *My child?*"

She nodded.

"You're having my child?"

"Are you angry?" she asked quickly.

"No. Of course not." He wasn't. He didn't know what he was except glad he was lying down. A child! He could scarcely believe it.

"Truly?" She laid a hand on his arm, still looking worried.

Luke smiled, shaking his head. "I'm not angry. I'm amazed. I never thought. When did you find out?"

"I knew that day."

His smile vanished. He stared. "The last day? The day we...made love?"

She nodded. "I'd been feeling sort of sick. I was late. I did one of those tests. It was positive."

He shoved himself up against the headboard and looked at her, anguished. "Why didn't you tell me?"

"How could I? You didn't want responsibility for anyone."

She didn't say the words accusingly, though he knew she had every right to feel that way. He rubbed a hand across his face.

"I'm sorry," he said hoarsely.

She touched her lips to his. "I'm not. You're here now. For all the right reasons."

"I might not have been," he argued, still stunned.

"Life isn't made of might haves, Luke. We both know that," she said softly. "Life is made of what actually happens. You're here. We love each other. That's what matters. Not all the things we should have done. Now is all we have. Now we go on from here."

He hesitated, almost afraid to ask. "Together?"

She kissed him. "Forever."

A shudder went through him. He drew her up against him and rubbed his forehead against her hair. "It sounds wonderful. Just keep reminding me, will you?"

"Every day," she promised, and bent her head, nestling it into the crook of his neck.

"Would you ever have told me?" he asked her when they'd made love once more. His mind was still trying to grapple with impending fatherhood.

He felt her shift against him. "Yes. After he was born." She touched his cheek and dropped a kiss on his chin. "A boy needs a father."

Luke swallowed. "It's a boy?"

Jill lifted her head and looked into his eyes. She smiled at him. "That's what they say."

He was born in April. A dark-haired, blue-eyed promise of spring. A lusty, seven-pound-nine-ounce gift of new life. They named him Keith.

*   *   *   *   *

Now that you've read about the two older Tanner brothers, don't miss brother #3's story—Noah's romance—in COWBOYS DON'T STAY. *It's due in December 1995 . . . only from Silhouette Desire!*

SILHOUETTE® Desire®

COMING NEXT MONTH

#943 THE WILDE BUNCH—Barbara Boswell

August's *Man of the Month,* rancher Mac Wilde, needed a woman to help raise his four kids. So he took Kara Kirby as his wife in name only....

#944 COWBOYS DON'T QUIT—Anne McAllister

Code of the West

Sexy cowboy Luke Tanner was trying to escape his past, and Jillian Crane was the only woman who could help him. Unfortunately, she also happened to be the woman he was running from....

#945 HEART OF THE HUNTER—BJ James

Men of the Black Watch

Fifteen years ago, Jeb Tanner had mysteriously disappeared from Nicole Callison's life. Now the irresistible man had somehow found her, but how could Nicole be sure his motives for returning were honorable?

#946 MAN OVERBOARD—Karen Leabo

Private investigator Harrison Powell knew beautiful Paige Stovall was hiding something. But it was too late—she had already pushed him overboard...with desire!

#947 THE RANCHER AND THE REDHEAD—Susannah Davis

The only way Sam Preston could keep custody of his baby cousin was to marry. So he hoodwinked Roni Daniels into becoming his wife!

#948 TEXAS TEMPTATION—Barbara McCauley

Hearts of Stone

Jared Stone was everything Annie Bailey had ever wanted in a man, but he was the one man she could *never* have. Would she risk the temptation of loving him when everything she cared about was at stake?

MILLION DOLLAR SWEEPSTAKES (III)

No purchase necessary. To enter, follow the directions published. Method of entry may vary. For eligibility, entries must be received no later than March 31, 1996. No liability is assumed for printing errors, lost, late or misdirected entries. Odds of winning are determined by the number of eligible entries distributed and received. Prizewinners will be determined no later than June 30, 1996.

Sweepstakes open to residents of the U.S. (except Puerto Rico), Canada, Europe and Taiwan who are 18 years of age or older. All applicable laws and regulations apply. Sweepstakes offer void wherever prohibited by law. Values of all prizes are in U.S. currency. This sweepstakes is presented by Torstar Corp., its subsidiaries and affiliates, in conjunction with book, merchandise and/or product offerings. For a copy of the Official Rules send a self-addressed, stamped envelope (WA residents need not affix return postage) to: MILLION DOLLAR SWEEPSTAKES (III) Rules, P.O. Box 4573, Blair, NE 68009, USA.

EXTRA BONUS PRIZE DRAWING

No purchase necessary. The Extra Bonus Prize will be awarded in a random drawing to be conducted no later than 5/30/96 from among all entries received. To qualify, entries must be received by 3/31/96 and comply with published directions. Drawing open to residents of the U.S. (except Puerto Rico), Canada, Europe and Taiwan who are 18 years of age or older. All applicable laws and regulations apply; offer void wherever prohibited by law. Odds of winning are dependent upon number of eligibile entries received. Prize is valued in U.S. currency. The offer is presented by Torstar Corp., its subsidiaries and affiliates in conjunction with book, merchandise and/or product offering. For a copy of the Official Rules governing this sweepstakes, send a self-addressed, stamped envelope (WA residents need not affix return postage) to: Extra Bonus Prize Drawing Rules, P.O. Box 4590, Blair, NE 68009, USA.

SWP-S895

Can an invitation to a bachelor auction,
a personal ad or a kiss-off bouquet
be the beginning of true love?

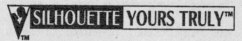

Find out in Silhouette's sexy, sassy new series
beginning in August

WANTED: PERFECT PARTNER
by Debbie Macomber

LISTEN UP, LOVER
by Lori Herter

Because we know just how busy you really are, we're
offering you a FREE personal organizer (retail value
$19.99). With the purchase of **WANTED: PERFECT
PARTNER** or **LISTEN UP, LOVER**, you can send in
for a FREE personal organizer! Perfect for your hustle-'n-
bustle life-style. Look in the back pages of the August
Yours Truly™ titles for more details.

And in September and October, *Yours Truly*™ offers
you not one but TWO proofs of purchase toward your
Pages & Privileges gifts and benefits.

So act now to receive your FREE personal organizer and
pencil in a visit to your favorite retail outlet and pick up
your copies of *Yours Truly*™.

Love—when you least expect it!

YTT2

As a *Privileged Woman,*
you'll be entitled to all these *Free Benefits.* And *Free Gifts,* too.

To thank you for buying our books, we've designed an exclusive FREE program called *PAGES & PRIVILEGES*™. You can enroll with just one Proof of Purchase, and get the kind of luxuries that, until now, you could only read about.

*B*IG HOTEL DISCOUNTS

A privileged woman stays in the finest hotels. And so can you—at up to 60% off! Imagine standing in a hotel check-in line and watching as the guest in front of you pays $150 for the same room that's only costing you $60. Your *Pages & Privileges* discounts are good at Sheraton, Marriott, Best Western, Hyatt and thousands of other fine hotels all over the U.S., Canada and Europe.

*F*REE DISCOUNT TRAVEL SERVICE

A privileged woman is always jetting to romantic places. When <u>you</u> fly, just make one phone call for the lowest published airfare at time of booking—<u>or double the difference back!</u> PLUS— you'll get a $25 voucher to use the first time you book a flight AND <u>5% cash back on every ticket you buy thereafter through the travel service!</u>

𝒯REE GIFTS!

A privileged woman is always getting wonderful gifts. Luxuriate in rich fragrances that will stir your senses (and his). This gift-boxed assortment of fine perfumes includes three popular scents, each in a beautiful designer bottle. <u>Truly Lace</u>...This luxurious fragrance unveils your sensuous side. <u>L'Effleur</u>...discover the romance of the Victorian era with this soft floral. <u>Muguet des bois</u>...a single note floral of singular beauty.

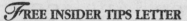

YOURS FREE!

$50 VALUE

𝒯REE INSIDER TIPS LETTER

A privileged woman is always informed. And you'll be, too, with our free letter full of fascinating information and sneak previews of upcoming books.

𝓜ORE GREAT GIFTS & BENEFITS TO COME

A privileged woman always has a lot to look forward to. And so will you. You get all these wonderful FREE gifts and benefits now with only one purchase...and there are no additional purchases required. However, each additional retail purchase of Harlequin and Silhouette books brings you a step closer to even more great FREE benefits like half-price movie tickets... and even more FREE gifts.

L'Effleur...This basketful of romance lets you discover L'Effleur from head to toe, heart to home.

Truly Lace... A basket spun with the sensuous luxuries of Truly Lace, including Dusting Powder in a reusable satin and lace covered box.

𝒞omplete the 𝓔nrollment 𝒯orm in the front of this book and mail it with this Proof of Purchase.

PROOF OF PURCHASE
Offer expires October 31, 1996

SD-PP4